JUMPER

JUMPER

MELANIE CROWDER

VIKING

VIKING
An imprint of Penguin Random House LLC, New York

First published in the United States of America by Viking, an imprint of Penguin
Random House LLC, 2022

Visit us online at penguinrandomhouse.com.

Library of Congress Cataloging-in-Publication Data is available.

Manufactured in Canada

ISBN 9780593326961

1 3 5 7 9 10 8 6 4 2

FRI
Edited by Liza Kaplan
Design by Ellice Lee

Text set in Baskerville

For Juniper

« « NOW « «

"FIRE IS NOT your friend."

I blink, confused, as my words cut through dead air. My voice
is raw, my throat shredded. I squint at the scuffed paint on the
walls, coarse industrial carpet, and pockmarked ceiling tiles—
everything's blurry, everything's gray. There's ash clumped in
what's left of my braid and smeared in a sooty paste down my
shirt. I'm as gray as the rest of it.

I don't even know why I'm talking—why I'd bother. I open
my mouth and a crack splits my chapped lips, stinging, slick with
fresh blood. I lick it away, though my tongue feels thick as a log,
and just as rough. "Fire can tear up the side of a mountain faster
than a grizzly. It can uproot a stand of trees and send them flying
through the air like hundred-foot javelins. It can swallow a town
whole. It may be the most beautiful thing you've ever seen, but fire
is not your friend."

My throat seizes and I clamp my mouth shut. I try to swallow, but that only makes me cough, hunched over and hacking into my filthy yellow sleeve. When I pull back, the fabric is flecked with gray—smoke and char still finding its way out of my lungs, along with shiny pearls of watery blood. I try to swallow again, but it burns. I could be at the bottom of a river and still my throat would be scorched, screaming for water.

I blink a couple of times—my eyes aren't working right either. Spots fizz and flare like campfire sparks. Everything's hazy. But I can feel the steel tabletop under my hands, so cold it burns the singed skin on my palms. The blunt edge of an aluminum chair digs into my hamstrings. I shift my feet—the ground is still there, solid, beneath my boots.

I blink again, but it's no good. The shadowy figure opposite me keeps splitting in two, then drifting back together like smoke trails that can't decide which updraft to follow. When the shadow starts talking, I blink some more, like that'll help sort the words into any kind of sense.

"I said I'll ask the questions."

Right. Officer Molt.

The shadow recedes and his dusty green uniform wavers into focus, then his face, so pale I can tell at one glance he's never seen so much as one day on the fire line. And that mustache, trimmed in a frown, with a gap of pink skin like an earthworm stuck to his top lip. If Jason were here to see this, the mustache alone would keep us entertained through a whole week of prescribed burns.

It slaps me like a bucket of ice water—why I'm really here in this sterile box, answering to Officer Mustache. The whisper-thin flame that's keeping me upright gutters and goes out, and I shake with cold or shock or both, rattling the folding chair beneath me. I drag a hand across the backs of my eyelids, then stare at the gnarled thing until I can make out the arc and bend of my own fingers. Earlier, I'd scrubbed until the skin bled, but there's still black under my cuticles and soot in the creases of my knuckles.

Officer Molt presses a button on the recording device and a red light flicks on. His eyebrows climb up his forehead, as if to say, *You know what this means, don't you?*

I do.

"State your name for the record."

"Blair Elizabeth Scott."

"Age?"

"Nineteen."

"What follows is a full account of the events leading up to the fourth of August."

I grunt, or maybe it's a growl. "Where should I start?"

All I get in response are those eyebrows again—he's not here to help me. No one is, not anymore. I'm too tired to argue; it's been at least thirty-six hours since I last slept.

The beginning, right?

But where *did* it all start? With Jason, of course. And Aunt Cate, too, I suppose, and all those doctors back home in Gunbarrel, and the shot crew, and the big Tahoe fire—trying to comb through where it all began is like untangling sooty knots at the base of my skull stirred up by sweat, dirt, smoke, and the constant pressure of my hardhat.

I don't know where to start, and I don't know what to wish— that Jason never came to live in our neighborhood? That I didn't ride past his house the day their moving truck pulled in? Or that I never saw a line of smokejumpers drop out of the sky?

« « BEFORE « «

Be alert. Keep calm. Think clearly. Act decisively.

STANDARD FIREFIGHTING ORDERS, NO. 6

CHAPTER 1

FOR A COUPLE of weeks as April tumbles into May, fits and bursts of rainfall wake Colorado's scrubby foothills. That startling green would catch anybody's attention—broken as it is by shards of cinnamon-colored rock and backed by show-offy white-tipped mountains and bluebird skies. But when you know it won't last long, when you know what's coming, you let your eyes linger, soaking up the riot of color while you can.

Even now, when all I want is to get out of here, it's hard to look away.

I rest my chin on my palm as the airplane banks, rising to get above the line of bumpy white thunderclouds building over the Front Range. Soon everything will turn brown and the whole state will hold its breath through a brittle summer, everybody hoping last winter's snows will be enough to keep the worst of the wildfires at bay.

They won't be, though. All signs point to a blistering fire

season. I scrape my bottom lip through my teeth, shifting in my seat. I can't wait.

The plane stops climbing, the engine settling into more of a buzz than a roar. The Rocky Mountains taper into wrinkly tan hummocks as Wyoming inches by far below, clefts of rock and stretches of barren plains sliding past.

Early this morning, my parents drove me to the airport. I guess we were a little sad? Mom's been sifting through boxes in the garage for weeks, sorting through tins of watercolors and reams of paper that have collected dust ever since her studio got nixed for a baby room just before I was born. Over the past few weeks, she's tried to hide her excitement at having a space of her own to work in again, but as the day of my departure loomed, her easels, brushes, and smocks made it first into the mudroom, then to the closet under the stairs, and finally, yesterday, into the nub of a hallway outside my bedroom door. So really, she didn't try *that* hard.

When it came time to say goodbye at the security line, though, the enormity of the moment seemed to suddenly catch up with Mom. Her voice warbled and choked, a rush of emotions making it impossible to understand a word she said. Dad had to take a work call halfway through our goodbyes. So I gave Mom a hug and an awkward pat on her shoulder, then I just sort of left.

Most of the seniors at my high school are treating this spring like one unending party—renting a flotilla of houseboats on Lake McConaughy every weekend from now through graduation. I'm pretty sure a few of them don't plan to sober up until at least July. Not me—I got special permission to take my end-of-year exams in April so I could get to Montana weeks before the end of school. I report to my hotshot crew Tuesday, and Jason is already at the compound, so I see no reason to hang around and torture myself with any more high school parties.

I lower the shade and rest my head against the stiff fabric of the seat back. No, I'm not sorry to be leaving.

"Folks, this is your pilot speaking. We've begun our initial descent into Missoula."

I rub the sleep from my eyes, check my watch, and slide up the shade. Cringing, I remove my forearm from the far side of the armrest, where it was pressed against the grandma sitting next to me. My shoulders are broad, and hard muscle strains the fabric over my arms and thighs; if I'm not consciously trying to take up less space, my bulk spreads into the next seat. I wouldn't want to be stuck next to me for a long flight.

I hug my arms across my chest and drop my forehead against the window to get a better look at the terrain. There's the Clark Fork snaking away to the south, I-90 cutting east to west through Missoula, and the woods outside of town where Aunt Cate lives.

Jason and I will technically be stationed at the hotshot compound up north—same one as last year—but we'll be moving all across the West, from one big fire to the next once the season ramps up. Two to three weeks on, then two days off, rinse and repeat. Anytime we're at all close, we'll stay with Aunt Cate on rest days, so really, we'll barely see those bunks.

It's a relief to be headed back to the same shot crew. It gets lonely out there, especially for the women. There are only ever a few of us and the guys can be real jerks about it. Most aren't afraid to say sexist shit to my face, so I can only imagine what they say when I'm not listening. But if Jason overhears that crap? *That* is one of the few things that make him act every bit as scary as he looks.

Truth is, the guys can have a bad day on the line, but if I'm anything less than perfect out there, they'll never look at me the same. Any level of trust or respect I might have built up will be gone. And that feeling—that you've always got to prove yourself, no matter how good you are—it can wear you down. So having my best friend with me out there isn't just a nice perk. It's what makes all the bullshit tolerable.

"The weather is a sunny seventy-eight degrees, with gentle winds out of the northwest. We hope you've enjoyed your trip; it's been a pleasure flying with you today."

The flight attendant gets on the mic to say something about

a credit card and reward miles; I turn my attention back to the view. As the plane makes its final turn, I catch a glimpse of the smokejumper base. Its signature white-and-red planes are parked on the tarmac, ready to drop a load of firefighters in the middle of nowhere. I sit up straight in my chair, craning for a better look.

Someday.

It feels like a hundred years before enough people move out of my way so I can shuffle off that plane, then another hundred for my gear to arrive at baggage claim—then I can finally walk through those automatic doors and outside. I heave a sigh of relief, adjust the brim of my McGuckin trucker hat, and lift my face to the sky. Montana air and Colorado air aren't all that different—it's a little wetter in Missoula—but even though I've spent more time there, *here* smells like home. Maybe it's the wide-open spaces that make the difference—how even when you're in the middle of town, it still feels like the edge of the wilderness.

Aunt Cate waits at the curb, leaning back against her Jeep, a glossy pair of aviators reflecting my goofy smile back at me. She sees me and kicks off the wheel well, wrapping me in a hug and clapping me on the back three times, hard, before letting go. I don't even try to stamp out the little spot fires flaring inside me. I'm back where I belong. *Finally.*

Aunt Cate starts up the Jeep. "It's good to see you, kid."

"You, too." I grin, tossing my gear bag in the back then climbing into the passenger seat.

"Jason's already at camp?"

"Yeah, his classes finished a few weeks ago, so he came up early to take his wilderness first aid course."

"You already did yours, what—two summers ago?"

"Yeah. It was awesome."

The laugh lines at the edges of her eyes and mouth crease white against her tanned skin. "Nerd."

"Says the biggest nerd I know."

"That's right," she says. "If you ask me, a person who doesn't completely nerd out about *something* in life must not care much about anything."

"Yeah, but most people aren't nerds about actual nerdy stuff like you."

Aunt Cate scoffs. "That classroom kind of learning is overrated."

She turns off the main road, shifts down, and we begin to climb into the hills. I drop my arm out the window, letting my fingers float along the trails of wind that spin over the Jeep's side mirror. My whole body relaxes—being in wild spaces always has that effect on me.

As we pass under the shadowed edge of the forest, a long sigh slides free. "I thought I'd never get out of there."

Aunt Cate tilts her head to the side, leaning into the hand propped on the door and letting her right hand steer around the lazy turns. "Sure seemed like that for a while there, didn't it?"

"Yeah. If I never set foot in Gunbarrel again, that'd be fine with me."

"Well . . ." She tucks a flyaway spiral of graying hair behind her ear. "You never know."

"What's that supposed to mean?"

Aunt Cate takes her time answering, like she does sometimes when she wants me to figure out for myself whatever it is she has to say. "I don't know what it's like to be a parent—I do know it's complicated. And I've seen enough families with sick kids to have an idea how hard that is, how it can change people. I know it felt oppressive for you sometimes—all that love and fear and desperation. But you're free now. And sometimes freedom changes everything."

She has a point. But I'm still not going home anytime soon.

I got really sick in fifth grade—that whole year was pretty much a blur of doctors' offices. I remember the shadows under my mom's eyes, and the way my dad used to pace the hall outside my bedroom at night, pausing to press his ear against the door every so often to make sure I was breathing.

I'd missed so much by the end of the year—when all my friends moved on to middle school, I stayed behind to redo fifth grade. And all those specialists were quick to hand out a list of activities I should refrain from participating in and precautions I should take, just to be safe.

Nothing gets under my skin like being told there's something I can't do.

The ribbon of road unspools before us as the Jeep chugs gradually upward. I breathe deep the scents of needles and sap, and of rich, dark soil, closing my eyes as the early summer air whips my hair into little cyclones, teasing it loose from its sloppy ponytail, and lapping the strands against my cheeks and eyelids and neck.

Aunt Cate lives by herself in a cabin in the middle of nowhere. It's up a winding Forest Service road where old-growth timber crowds the edges of the pavement. Then you take an unmarked dirt road even farther into the woods until the A-frame's red peak pokes through the trees. The metal roof was Aunt Cate's idea, because she didn't want to have to climb up there after a heavy snowfall and rake the stuff off. And the patio was my idea, seeing as how a log cabin in the middle of the forest is just as likely to go up in flames as the trees, unless it has defensible space around the perimeter.

She may have rolled her eyes and said that since the patio was my idea, I could haul and lay the flagstone myself. But once I was done, she installed sprinklers facing away from the house, toward the undergrowth all around—so all my yammering about the wildland–urban interface must have convinced her some.

Aunt Cate's a biomedical engineer—so damn smart she doesn't have to be anywhere near the hospital—she's got a lab set up in the extra bedroom where she develops medical tech for use in clinical trials. They pay her a ton of money and give her nearly everything she asks for just to keep her from leaving. And maybe because she doesn't have kids of her own, or because she doesn't trust people back home to do right by me, or maybe to give Mom a break, she's flown me up to Montana to spend summers with her every year since fifth grade (the first time around).

That's how I got started fighting fires. The station by Aunt Cate's is staffed by volunteers—hardly anyone lives way out there, so I took a turn on a fire crew well before I was technically old enough to qualify. They wouldn't have stood for my being in any real danger, but even a ten-year-old can be trusted to dig a line with a dull-enough Pulaski.

Somehow, Aunt Cate knew I needed to get out into the woods and sweat, to dig a line in the soil and watch the work of my own body, weak as it was, stop a wildfire in its tracks. Somehow, she knew what I needed wasn't a list of things I couldn't or shouldn't do. I needed to come face-to-face with proof of my own strength.

Over the course of those summers, Aunt Cate taught me how to tie a fly and set a trap, how to make a fire in a rainstorm, and how to fend for myself in the wilderness for days on end—the polar opposite of life back home, with my parents hovering over my every move, freaking out every time my face got even a little red.

Aunt Cate and I went fishing most weeks during my summers in Montana, and hunting as soon as the season opened. We even flew to Alaska once to spend two weeks in a black cloud of mosquitoes, tracking mountain goats up the side of a cliff. I've never been afraid of heights, which is probably one reason I got myself into this mess.

Wildland Fire Crew Types

contract: Privately staffed wildland firefighters; crews can
be called upon to supplement those supplied by federal
agencies.

helitack: Crews that can be deployed quickly via helicopter to
provide wildfire response, tactical support, or emergency
medical assistance.

hotshot: Elite wildland firefighters utilized primarily for
initial attack; usually a twenty-person crew consisting
of a superintendent, assistant superintendent, squad
leaders, senior firefighters, and temporary employees.

rappeller: Elite wildland firefighters utilized for initial attack
on large fires; transported to fire via helicopter with
descent to the ground via rappel.

smokejumper: Elite wildland firefighters; utilized primarily
to suppress small fires in remote areas best accessed by
aircraft transport and parachute deployment.

CHAPTER 2

WE WAKE UP early the next morning to get in a long hike following the deer trails behind Aunt Cate's house. She sets her usual quick pace, her mincing steps twice as fast as mine. The air is cool, sharp with the scent of pine needles and rising sap, the soil loose and crumbling from the weight of winter's wet snows. It feels good to move, to let go of all that pent-up energy and let my stride stretch long and loose.

After our hike, a quick abs-and-arms circuit, a brisk shower, and a heaping lunch, Aunt Cate pores over my most recent medical records and readouts and then lectures me about nutrition, hydration, and constant, meticulous monitoring, as if I don't already know my life depends on it. She hands me a new pocket-sized notebook, extracting a promise that I'll fill every damn page, and carefully, too. Once she's convinced, we pile back into the Jeep and she drives me up north to the hotshot compound.

When she pulls into the drive, she gives me one of her looks, long and hard, then one of her hugs, long and hard, too, until she's satisfied I understand the rest—the love that goes hand in hand with her protectiveness.

From her? Yeah, I definitely do.

I wave goodbye to Aunt Cate, heft my pack, and go to the office to check in with Vick. He's never bothered to hide his annoyance at my presence. At all. Last season during training, he scoffed at the idea that—as a teenager and a girl—I'd even have a chance at making a hotshot crew in my first season. But I proved myself in those early weeks with top scores on the fitness tests. I didn't wash out, and neither did Jason. And maybe Vick likes training rookies even less than accommodating females. Maybe. These past few years, recruitment numbers are down among elite crews, so if you're fit, tough, and smart, age isn't the barrier it used to be. Besides, our superintendent, Pete, who handpicks his own crew, was impressed, which is all that mattered in the end.

Vick raises an eyebrow when I rap on his office doorframe.

"Blair Scott, checking in!" I try not to sound perky. I really do.

He rifles through a stack of folders, still uncomfortable behind a desk even though he got promoted to the job decades ago. "Everything's here—annual medical exam, rehire paperwork— you're good to go."

Nice to see you, too. "I'll just head to the barracks, then?"

Vick jaws his usual wad of Nicorette gum. "Hope you kept up

on your fitness. Temps are set to spike next week."

"Early start to the season, then?" Hey, this is almost like a conversation between friends or coworkers or—

He gestures to the door with a grunt. "We'll know soon enough."

Okay, so not really a conversation.

I duck out the door, nearly colliding with Pete, who nods in greeting. "Training begins at oh-six-hundred."

"Got it!"

He gives a thumbs-up in return—as enthusiastic a response as I'm ever going to get. Pete may be gruff, but once you've earned his respect, you've got it.

On my way to the barracks, I spot Wolf, my favorite of the senior firefighters. He drops from the pull-up bar and spits a wad of chew in the trash. "Hey, Blair! You're back."

"I'm back!"

I spin in a giddy circle, my bags flying wide, laughing for no reason except I'm so relieved to finally be here. When I quit spinning like a fool and my gear slams back against my sides, there's Walt, lounging against the barrack doors, blocking my way in. Well, shit. Last season, he was the other rookie besides Jason and me to make it onto our hotshot crew. I'd hoped he transferred to another crew. No such luck, apparently.

"Hi, Walt."

"Blair." He grimaces in return. "Still haven't figured out that women don't belong in fire?"

That whole thing about blood boiling—around Walt, I can believe it, easy. I force out a laugh. "Did you take that comedy act on the road over the winter?"

I brush past him, though what I really want is to make his nose run red. There were three of us women last season. Nora made it clear that she wouldn't be coming back. All the guys may not be as in your face about it as Walt, but there are a thousand little ways we're made to feel unwelcome out there. Nora is a badass. And funny as hell, but she doesn't love fire like me—at least, not enough to tolerate all the sexist bullshit. The other woman, Amy, took a position on a crew in Washington. She and I never hit it off—she's so busy trying to convince the guys that she isn't "one of those girls," she doesn't even realize the shit she eats for breakfast every day. You do what you have to to survive a career in fire—I get it. I just don't like it.

I fling open the barracks door and stroll inside. *I belong here,* I remind myself. Every bit as much as the guys. And with everything I put up with to get here and stay here, I've more than earned my place.

When I spot Jason, the rest is forgotten. He's sprawled on his bunk, writing a letter home, probably—either to his little brother Willie or to his on-again, off-again ex-girlfriend Janie. He's rattling the pen against the notebook, raking his messy blond waves out of his eyes with the other hand. Jason looks like a little kid, nibbling on the corner of his lip in concentration. And then he spots me—a grin takes over his whole face. I drop my things on the next bunk over, taking a swipe at that pretty-boy hair.

"Hey!" He chucks his stationery to the side.

I laugh in response, so damn happy, backing up a few steps as he comes barreling into the aisle. We hop around for a minute in a half back-slapping hug, half wrestling match before sinking back onto our separate bunks.

"Dude," he says, kicking the underside of my boot. "You made it."

"Ahhhhhhh." I collapse onto the bed, my arms flung out to the sides. I tilt my head so I can see his face. "We may still be lowly scrapes at the back of the line, but I'll take it!"

"Yep." He grins. "Although *technically*, I'm a transfer from my winter posting, so I'm not even a temporary hire."

I roll my eyes. "Dude thinks he's *sooooo* fancy after *one* winter season."

Really, I'm jealous, and we both know it. I would've traded my last year of high school in a snap for a year studying fire science at Front Range Community College and a winter posting with the Forest Service.

"That I am." He flexes, hamming it up. "Extremely fancy."

Jason's jacked—he was an all-state linebacker. He's got heavy eyebrows and chiseled cheekbones—a natural resting bitch face. But those cheeks get all round and doughy when he breaks into a smile, and really, if you knew him even a little, you'd see he's a softy, underneath it all.

Jason could have gotten a football scholarship to a Pac-12 school, but who wants to chase a ball that doesn't even roll properly when you could be out in the woods chasing wildfire? At least, that's what I always say—enough times to convince even him, I suppose.

Okay, so those of us who run toward fire instead of away from it like most sane human beings do—well, we're definitely a little nuts. But we're also pretty damn meticulous, so all that training and some good preparation kicks in along with the adrenaline. Naturally, we'll be put through our paces—a full two weeks of classroom and field training before they let us loose on a real fire.

After that we'll be ready. Impatient as I am to get going, I need that time to double-check my numbers at that high-exertion level. But my head's already there—I've been waiting for this fire season since the last one ended. Really, it feels like I've been waiting for this forever.

Wildland Firefighting Tools

chainsaw: Gas-powered saw used to down trees and clear
brush in the wildfire's path.

crosscut saw: Manual saw used perpendicular to the trunk
of a tree; operated by two firefighters in a side-to-side
motion.

drip torch: Gas-powered incendiary device used to burn
flammable material before it can become fuel for a
wildfire.

mcleod: Half rake, half hoe; used by handcrews to construct a
fire line.

Pulaski: Half ax, half adze; used by handcrews to construct a
fire line.

CHAPTER 3

WE'RE IN CHARGE of our own physical training on a hot-shot crew, and I love being paid to work out on the days when we aren't working sixteen-hour shifts on a fire. After a run and a quick session in the weight room, Jason and I toss our camping chairs onto the grass behind the ready room where the buildings block the compound's exterior lights. My body feels good—ready for the season, and damn, am I pumped to be here. Jason unpacks his ukulele—a tenor size so his fat fingers don't buzz the chords. I snap my harmonica out of a pouch at my hip and lean back, taking in the stars and a pearly-white moon. It's our little ritual, whenever we find ourselves in a camp civilized enough for small musical instruments.

"You see the doctor before your flight?"

"Of course."

Jason looks purposefully away. He can switch from talking about football or crude crew humor to serious shit on a dime.

That real stuff scares the crap out of me and he knows it; he gives me the space to fidget and squirm without an audience.

"What about Aunt Cate? Does she think you can handle a long season?"

"Yeah." Seriously. Hashing out this argument all winter long wasn't enough for him? "I'm fine."

"You're not *fine*. You're strong as hell and tougher than anyone I've ever met, but everybody has limitations. So your body is yours? Ignoring that isn't going to make it go away."

"I can manage it." Why does everyone feel the need to talk me out of the one thing I want?

"At least reconsider telling Pete? You proved yourself to him last season—he knows how good you are. He'll work with you."

"Can't take that risk, especially since I wasn't up front about it before."

"Blair. Come on. You're going to have to trust somebody sometime."

"I trust you." My voice wavers and cracks. It isn't easy for me to admit that I need anything from anyone, even Jason.

"And what about if I'm not here—if I get transferred to another crew or dispatched to a different fire? I can't always be your second set of eyes." He turns to look at me then, half of his face draped in shadow. "What if I can't do it anymore—what if the day comes when I can't keep your secrets?"

It's suddenly hard to swallow. Hard to breathe, for that matter. But he'd never do it—I know that. Jason would never give up on me.

"Like I said, I trust you." I yank up a fistful of grass and chuck it at him. "Anyway, I trust you to quit yammering and start strumming before I leave you here alone in the dark."

Jason grunts, not bothering to hide his disappointment. So I can't wear my emotions on my sleeve like him. That's nothing new.

He picks up his uke and begins plucking away. I am no musical prodigy, so Jason always plays everything in the same key as the harmonica. I honk and wheeze along to whatever he strums—Nathaniel Rateliff or Beyoncé or his favorite, Billy Joel—more for the company than any musicality I might add to the mix. Once Jason really gets going, I dip my head back, letting the harmonica fall, forgotten, into my lap while I watch the stars punch holes in the darkness, one pinprick at a time.

That feeling—freedom and friendship and being dwarfed by the wide wilderness—it's everything to me.

Jason and I met when I was in fifth grade—the second time around. There were plenty of reasons I stuck out—the special diets my mom was always trying out on me, the heart monitor I wore strapped to my chest for a month straight, and all the times I got called down to the nurse's office to take some medication or another. Since I towered over the rest of the kids, most of them didn't pick on me. Except for Donny Reasel. The first time he called me *Sicky Snotty, Blair Scotty*, I wound up and punched him in the nose so hard, he squealed like a pig. Bled like one, too.

I'd never hit anybody before, and man, did I get in trouble. For weeks afterward, the dinnertime conversation was all about how *violence never solves anything* and *the pen is mightier than the sword*. Well, little Donny Reasel figured out quick that I wasn't allowed to hit him anymore, so that shit stain became my torturer. Every single day, he and his friends would wait for me to walk by, then follow two steps behind, taunting me the whole way to school.

It was all going great for them until one sunny Saturday when Jason moved to Gunbarrel. We were instant friends even though he was a year ahead of me in school. We had identical *Revenge of the Sith* lunch boxes, which is the sort of thing controversial enough to bond you for life. On the way to the bus stop that Monday morning, when Donny and his friends tried the same routine, I took it like always, walking away like my windbreaker could repel their nursery-rhyme-level insults.

But Jason didn't. He turned around slowly to face them, his swinging lunch box suddenly gone still. Donny's jeering smile began to slip, sure he was in for another bloody nose. But Jason only took one more step toward him, leaned in, and said something in a low voice. After that, Donny Reasel never so much as looked at me. Apparently, my parents were right about all that *words have the power to move mountains* stuff. When it comes to people like Jason, anyway.

After that, we were best friends, no matter what. Forever.

Fire Watch-Out Situations

No. 2: In country not seen in daylight.

CHAPTER 4

THREE WEEKS LATER, after our required training is complete and our crew has been put through every kind of fitness test, team-building drill, and pack-out exercise you can imagine, our season really begins. On a balmy Wednesday afternoon, a fire cloud forms to the north, underscored with orangey-brown smudges from the flames below. It's big, and close. So even though any number of crews are surely being called in from around the region, Jason and I hustle to join our crew, combing through packs and sharpening tools. I've got my GPS and compass, a headlamp and an extra hairband, my shelter and shroud, and my boots, plus snacks stashed into every empty nook. My canteens are full and my tools are sharp. I'm ready to go.

Pete nods once in satisfaction when he finds us all prepping to leave before the call has even come in. "The Lolo and Chief Mountain crews were called over the weekend to Nevada,

Bitterroot is en route to southern California, and Helena just left for North Dakota. This one's ours."

I pull on my flame-resistant Nomex—a standard-issue yellow shirt, but custom-ordered green pants. The ones the Forest Service gives us are made to fit a man and will chafe the inside of a woman's legs to bleeding inside of a week on the fire line. So yeah, I splurge on pants that fit. And wool socks. Hotshot crews do a hell of a lot of hiking, and we go long stretches without seeing any laundry service. A few pairs of durable socks are gold. I splurged on some good boots, too. Shot crews are on their feet for long-ass days you've got to have good boots.

"Weather report didn't mention lightning strikes," Wolf says quietly as he sharpens the teeth on his chainsaw.

"Yeah," Pete grunts. "There are few enough of them this early in the season that the jumpers would have been all over that."

I wince. "Campfire, then?"

Fire bans are posted at every campground in the state, but people can be unaccountably dumb. Sometimes, when campers start a fire, they're so ashamed, they get the hell out of there and don't tell a soul. If they'd only call it in the first second they're able, fire crews could jump on it before it blows up.

"Some dumbass probably tossed a lit cigarette out the window." Jason rolls his eyes, cranking the seal on his canteen.

I kick out my legs, flexing and relaxing my quads, trying

to shake that itchy feeling all over that always comes when I'm waiting for a call. It's nothing more than chemicals: adrenaline, cortisol, dopamine. But it feels like fire licking up and down my arms and legs, warming me up for the two-foot, ten-foot, fifty-foot flames I might face.

Pete lifts the blade of his Pulaski up to his eye and sights down the edge. "There were no scheduled burns in that draw that could have gotten out of control, so this one shouldn't be our fault."

Jason grimaces but doesn't say any more as he shifts the weight in his pack so it won't rub wrong if we have a long hike. Those heavy brows of his always look a little scary, but when he's focused on something—before a football game or a big test or, like now, getting ready for a fire, they snap together, all dark and stormy.

He turns his back to the others and ducks his head close to mine. "Your numbers good?"

I nod. "Ready for anything."

He smirks at that. "Cocky as ever."

"I'm just that good." I shrug, going for nonchalant.

"So you say."

I cackle, and the creases between his brows ease.

Pete's radio sends out a stream of orders and we leap to our feet, slinging our packs over our shoulders and running toward the crew buggies. Across the parking lot, a few guys whoop and whistle. Everybody's different in that moment—some get amped, while others go into stealth mode. I may look pretty calm, but those flames are licking clear to my throat, all those chemicals itching to be let loose.

We pile in to the buggies. I sit across the aisle from Jason, the familiar bulk of him enough to put me at ease. I slap my hand down on his knee and he leans out and bumps my shoulder. *Finally.*

The buggy roars up the road, leaving the compound far behind. In the back, we sway with the bends in the winding mountain roads, while our gear rattles in the racks above. The farther north we travel, the more the traffic thins out—nobody else is driving toward the fire. The few cars we pass are flying, rushing to get out of the way. Along the road, towering evergreens blur together in an almost audible hum.

We pull up just short of the fire and everybody tumbles out, throwing on their hardhats and gloves. I glance around once my boots hit the ground, getting my bearings. We're in a dense section of forest tapering off to a rocky hillside that's little more than one wrinkle in a range of overlapping ridges. The air is full of smoke already, the metallic notes settling at the back of my throat.

There's no long hike in to get to the fire, meaning we'll have plenty of support this time. When you have to leave engines and dozers behind, when you're nowhere near a stream, or when the air cover can't get to you to drop a bucket of water or a line of slurry, well-tended gardening tools are all you've got. Saws, axes, rakes, and hoes—against a wildfire. Plus your brain and your brute strength and every last bit of grit you can call up.

Pete plants the butt of his Pulaski like a flag in the dirt. "The main fire is going to run up and down those hills like lightning, so don't even think about moving any closer. We're going to work in the flats right here and dig a line straight to that rock outcropping. We'll use that as an anchor point, see if we can hold this flank."

He glances at the sky. "Weather report calls for a gusty day."

"No shit," Jason mutters, eyeing the smoke whipping past in the gaps in the canopy.

"If the fire continues on its path east, we're good to let it burn for a while. But we cannot let it jump our line and start moving south, toward town. Our exits are back along the road we drove in on, or down the creek on the other side of those rocks. If the wind shifts, wrapping the west flank of the fire around behind us, we're going to have to cut and run, and quick. So keep an eye on your buddy, and stay close."

Pete nods once after he hears confirmation from each of us and double-checks that the crew radios are all set to the correct channel. We settle into our line and dig in. Hotshot crews tend to be highly ordered; everybody is in their same spot every time. Fire lines are precise down to the inch, and the tool order never varies. But everybody has their own way of working. Some are like sprinters—a mad dash followed by gusting breaks. Others are more like distance runners, slow and steady. I'm somewhere in the middle, I suppose, but I never turn my back on the main fire, not if I can help it.

I want to see it coming.

At the front are the sawyers with their chainsaws in a constant rev and roar, clearing any of those big trees that could topple in the wrong direction if they catch, throwing the fire beyond our line. Jason and I work Pulaskis, biting deep into the dirt. Swing, step. Swing, step. It's monotonous, punishing work—the tools are heavy and the ground is hard as rocks—but I love it.

A couple of transfers from the Lolo shot crew come behind us with mcleods, hacking at the exposed roots, then hoeing the hardscrabble all the way down to mineral soil. Walt brings up the rear, raking everything we till up back a couple feet. Last season, Jason and I were at the end of the line, the newest and greenest members of the crew. We may not have moved far up, but we've moved.

The buzz of saws pauses, and the swampers call for help clearing the slash. We stow our tools and begin dragging the logs and spindly branches well clear of our line. I raise my eyes to the ridge. When we first arrived, the sky looked no different from any hazy summer day. But now the clouds are darkening, turning a sickly yellow, and thickening with ash. Our crew always works fast. But when you can't see even a scrap of blue in the sky, you find another gear.

Adrenaline. Cortisol. Dopamine.

My undershirt is soaked through. I knot a bandana over my forehead to keep the sweat from dripping into my eyes and go back for another armful of brush. As the haze thickens, I glance back along our exits and over to the rocks that will be our emergency shelter-in-place location if it comes to that. By the time I drop my load and turn back, flames break out on top of the ridge.

My chest goes tight, like a winch turning in on itself, cranking hard. I tuck my chin, releasing a long exhale as I glance sidelong at Jason. A slow smile spreads across his face, to match the one tugging at my lips. I reach around to the back of my hardhat and velcro a shroud of fabric across my nose and mouth—it's no fun breathing hard with a thick layer of cloth covering your mouth, but I learned years ago to protect my lungs from the smoke. Another deep breath. It steadies the nerves jangling along every inch of me.

"Here we go," Jason mutters.

"It's about time." I flex my fingers, then grip the long wooden handle of my Pulaski.

The fire is quiet still, a distant roar. Orange spears taste the clouds, churning the air with wave after wave of heat, singeing the sky as flames roll over the ridge. The downhill will slow it, but that fire is coming our way.

I set my teeth, gauging the distance and speed of the main fire, and the time it would take me and Jason to reach the safety zone. I force down a series of cooling breaths and a couple swigs of water. I have to keep my stress levels low—staying calm is not optional.

Pete calls the crew over. "Time to tie this into the black."

Sometimes you have to fight fire with fire—burn everything between your fire line and the advancing flames. Sometimes the monster you create can beat down the monster coming your way. But other times, it can turn on you—jump the line or get whipped into a frenzy by changing winds—and the next thing you know, you've got fire on both sides, closing off your only way out.

One by one, we stow our tools and grab the drip torches we stashed. The wildfire is still coming, trailing a swath of blackened forest behind it like some goth bridal veil. All along my skin, that chemical fire flickers and dances—I love dragging fire. But at times like this, when you do it out of self-defense, to stop the wildfire from rolling over you, it's a scary sort of thrill.

"Light it up," Pete hollers over his shoulder.

Together, we walk the perimeter, dripping a ragged trail of flame that quivers and leaps across the ground, rushing to meet the wildfire. My breath comes hard and fast as the flames I set sear and snap at the air. Heat sizzles the length of me, burrowing between seams and coating my skin.

Fire is slower moving downhill than up, so our backfire catches up to the wildfire more than halfway up the ridge. Flame meets flame in a deafening clash of popping pitch and cracking gusts. Once the fuel between us and the big fire is consumed, once we've established a safe zone of smoldering char, I tuck away my torch. Inside me, those chemical flames die down, too, down to gleaming coals storing up heat for the next rush.

I straighten my pack and begin scraping over the line again. After a backfire, you work the border between the char that the fire ate up and spat out and the green, unburnt fuel. In any other situation, you'd want to be over there, in all that fresh growth. But when wildfire is all around, you want to be where there's nothing more to burn. So you work with one foot in the black and one foot in the green. One foot in life, one foot in death.

Half of the crew steps into the smoldering meadow to shovel dirt over shin-high flames, advancing like wraiths in a steady line, the ground steaming all around them, smoke curling to fill their boot prints. Darkness descends and the air cools. In the distance, orange flames spit sparks and launch firebrands like short-range meteors shooting across the night sky.

It's midnight before the last flames flicker out. I'm so beat, I want to lie down right there in the scorched dirt. Instead, Jason and I join the others combing through the char, checking for hot spots. We get halfway through the meadow when a replacement crew shows up to take over. We stumble back to the road, more than happy to let them finish the mop-up. And then we're asleep in a sooty huddle before the buggy even makes it out to the highway.

Atypical Wildfire

backfire: A fire suppression tactic in which crews deliberately set fire to an area in order to reduce available fuel for an advancing wildfire.

burnover: When an advancing fire overwhelms a wildland firefighter's position; an emergency situation often requiring deployment of a fire shelter.

let-burn: A predetermined area where firefighters will not attempt to suppress a wildfire either for the benefit of the ecosystem or out of a scarcity of resources.

CHAPTER 5

AT THE END of the week, when we get a much-needed day off, Jason and I check out, pile into his truck, and head into town. He's a Billy Joel guy—no matter how much I may roll my eyes, it's impossible to listen without singing along. I'm so beat after a week on that fire that I give in to the goofy smile and catchy choruses.

We hit the rec center first. Normal people may ignore the notice to shower before they get in the pool, but if anyone on a wildland crew did that, the water would end up with a scuzzy layer of soot on top, and we'd never be let back in the place. Once I'm clean by city standards, I plop into the hot tub, hissing. Jason's already in there, groaning about his pulverized biceps and lats.

I lean back, slowly, balancing so the knots at the base of my skull have a chance at loosening up. "Giant steaks with a round of jalapeño poppers to start?"

"Pizza for me. Then more pizza."

"Followed by tater tots smothered in green chile sauce."

"Deal."

I shift so the jets can get to work on that spot between my shoulder blades that always ties itself up.

Jason sinks deeper into the water. "Tell me again why we didn't go get cushy summer jobs at McGuckin or the tree farm or punching tickets at a movie theater?"

I snort. McGuckin. It'd take Jason all of twenty minutes to get bored working in a hardware store.

"No, seriously. Just think—air-conditioning. Civilized eight-hour shifts. With breaks. Not even a hint of mortal danger."

"Shut up. You love this—don't even pretend otherwise."

"Yeah." A sly smile creeps over his face. "I do. Hey, should we try to get a posting in California over the winter? They've got fires pretty much year-round."

"And ditch Aunt Cate?"

"We could come back here for the summer. You know you want to rack up days on initial attack."

He's got a point. "You know in Cali they've got goats to keep the grasses in the hills cropped short. If you can't find a job at a wildland station, you could always hit up the goatherds for a winter gig."

Jason lashes out, dunking my head underwater. I'm still laughing when I come up for air, sputtering and snorting water out of my nose. I slap the top of the water with the flat of my hand, sending a sheet directly into his face.

"Truce!" he yells.

"I thought so." Still, I glide to the opposite wall where I'll have plenty of warning if he changes his mind.

We stay in the hot tub until our muscles are soupy, then hit the showers a second time. My hair is thick as a horsetail, so I usually keep it in a braid or two to slot through the straps in my hardhat. It helps with the tangles a bit, but still I scrub shampoo through my hair three times, until even the smell of smoke is gone.

A dozen of the guys from our crew are already at the diner on Main Street by the time we get there. The owner gives us a free platter of fries and hot wings for the table and a pile of tokens so we can play pinball and darts all evening. The older wildland guys get free beer down at the bar on the corner—most people in town treat us hotshots like honored guests. After all, we're the ones keeping fires from ripping through town; a little free stuff is basically a down payment for the day when we're called to hold that line.

When I step up to the counter to order, I can barely put together a coherent sentence—the girl in the U of M ball cap working the cash register is so damn pretty. Not like it matters; she doesn't even see me. Her eyes go all soft, straight to Jason. He sidles up beside me, an easy grin spreading across his face. When she starts twirling the end of her ponytail between her fingers, I duck away, my cheeks surely red as a vat of pizza sauce.

What can I say? Jason and I always fall for the same girls, and ninety-nine times out of a hundred, it's him they want. Scratch that—not ninety-nine—one hundred percent of the time. I can't blame them, not really. If I were interested in guys, even a little, I'd probably join them.

I've learned over the years not to get my hopes up, not when Jason is around, anyway. So I leave him there to flirt with the girl at the counter and head to the row of arcade games at the back. There is a line three rednecks deep for Big Buck Hunter, so I pick the X-Men pinball machine in the corner with blinking red lights where Jean Grey's pupils should be, the smoke that curls in the air behind her shaped almost like wings. I draw the lever back and fire, losing myself in the clicking and rolling and that shiny devil of a silver ball. Steak, then wings, then jalapeño poppers, all with my best friend. So what if I never have a girlfriend? It isn't a bad lineup for a night off.

Three hundred miles to the south, a carful of hungover campers pack up their tents and folding chairs, kick crumpled beer cans into a pile, and chuck them in the trunk in a haphazard mess to sort out when they get home. (Or when their heads stop pounding the following day, more likely.) The campfire quit smoking long ago, so without so much as a backward glance at the loose circle of stones that served as a fire ring, they pull away.

If even one of them would have reached out a hand close to the ashes, they would have felt the heat smoldering below. If they would have directed a kick at the charred dirt, they might have seen still-glowing coals beneath the ashes. They might have dumped the swill of ice water from the cooler over the coals—or pissed on it, at the very least.

But they don't.

An evergreen forest is meant to withstand a passing fire if the flames don't reach the crown. But when there is too much dead material on the forest floor—rotten limbs, decaying stumps, and brush everywhere you look—that fire is going to burn too hot. If the trees start torching, tossing flame back and forth up in the canopy, it's only a matter of time before an abandoned campfire becomes a hundred-, thousand-, hundred-thousand-acre fire. If it really blows up, there's no stopping it, not until rain or snow buries it for good.

And this one has the makings of a very big fire.

CHAPTER 6

AFTER A 4:00 a.m. call, our hotshot crew is driven to a big fire camp that the logistics folks are still hustling to get set up along the Montana-Wyoming border. Before I turned eighteen, I spent my summers working camp crews, loading and unloading enough gear and food and laundry supplies to service the whole operation. It was as close to fire as I could get, aside from the volunteer station and a lucky stint on a contract crew when I wasn't technically old enough yet.

But now? I'm not just setting up camp so others can attack the fire. I'm the one heading out on the fire.

By midweek, the blaze spreads into the park. Yellowstone is rugged country, and while there isn't much wildland-urban interface to worry about, there's still park infrastructure, and protected wildlife, and something of our national image rolled into that place. Pete checks in our crew while we set up camp at the shady end of the meadow, then everybody gathers around for a quick briefing. "There's a good fire break in place along this flank—some paved sections of road, and a couple creeks and rivers. Our job is to clear the gaps between them. This is a big fire, so we'll want a wide line." He smiles ruefully. "There won't be any glory for us this time—we're far away from the really hot spots. But this line *has* to hold, which is why *we're* here instead of some second-rate rookie crew."

"Oh, joy," Jason deadpans as he settles his pack over his shoulders. "At least we won't have to worry about PT this week."

"Speak for yourself," I say.

"Come on, Blair." Then, in a low voice, "Don't overdo it."

He's right—he usually is. But as a rule, I have to work twice as hard as the guys. He knows that, in his head, but he doesn't *get* it. I don't know that any of them could. "I'm still doing abs and arms every night before bed."

Jason sighs, hefting his Pulaski and adjusting his gloves. "Of course you are."

By the third day in camp, we're still cutting line and clearing fuel while crews on the other flank attack the fire. We're not seeing any real action yet, so Jason and I have settled into our little routine. The rest of the crew pretty much eats and falls asleep, since that next shift starts ticking closer the minute the last one ends and sleep becomes more important than just about anything else.

But I have to pack on extra calories—no choice there—so I can't sleep just yet. I don't mind much; even fifteen minutes laughing under the stars with Jason makes the whole hard day worth it. So when we spill out of the buggies at the end of each shift, we wash our disgusting hands and sweaty, sooty faces, then grab dinner number one—whatever is quick, like a prewrapped burrito, steak hoagie, or tuna melt.

We take our grab-and-go dinner from the tractor trailer made over as a camp kitchen and head to the meadow, where we sit in the grass and wolf it down. Then, and only then, do we head to our tents to grab a change of clothes and hit the showers, soaping all over at least three times to get the worst of the grime off. I learned last season that the shampoo the Forest Service supplies is no good for hair longer than a buzz cut, so that's another thing I splurge on. That and the leave-in conditioner I brought from home so I have a fighting chance at getting a comb through the tangles. Back in high school, I thought the snarls that formed under my ponytail after a cross-country meet were bad, but that was nothing compared to the mat caused by sooty wind rolling off a wildfire.

Once we're clean, Jason and I go back to the meal tent for a second dinner, hobbit style. For that pass, I take the time to make something from the salad and burger bars. You burn a crazy amount of calories working a sixteen-hour shift on a fire line; if you're shy about shoveling those calories back in your body, you'll be skinny as a rail by the end of the season. And worse, you won't have the energy to do the work that's asked of you. You just won't. The sack lunches we're handed before each shift are at least four thousand calories, but even that isn't enough some days.

After dinner, we waddle back to our tents, bellies out, groaning under the weight of everything we just ate. Setting up in a big fire camp is a luxury for hotshots. Other people cooking your food. Showers and a medical tent. Laundry service. Might as well be the Ritz-Carlton compared with what we're used to—sleeping in the middle of nowhere, most times without even a tent in order to cut weight, with no real way to get clean. The shitty thing about down time on big fires is all the guys from other crews. Their eyes on my body are worse than the sweaty, ashy grime that coats my skin at the end of the day. And I can't wash it off, not ever.

Jason and I find a spot out of the way, pull out our camping chairs, and set them up with a view of the moon rising over the trees. I settle in, dropping my head back as the lights over the meal tent flick off. The wind shifts, blowing the smoke south, so the night sky can show off. Not like when you're a hundred miles away from the nearest streetlight and it seems like there's more stars than sky up there, but clear enough so the Milky Way splatters across the dark. Jason grabs his uke; I wipe down my harmonica. He sends out a spray of notes, those meaty fingers dancing around the fretboard like that's where they belong. His face goes all silly—a look most people don't see. Beneath the first impression of his stocky frame and resting bitch face, Jason's really a softy. A complete goofball.

"You think we'll ever see some action on this fire?" He pinches the thumb and pointer finger of his strumming hand together and trills between the A and E strings.

I drop my hands onto my legs so I can rub out a tight spot along my right IT band. "Nah, not this time. They'll have it mopped up before it gets anywhere close to our position."

Jason's left hand dances over the strings in something like a melody, one I could pick out anywhere; he plays the same one anytime he's thinking about Janie.

"You've got to let her go, dude."

Jason grunts, but doesn't switch to a different song. He and Janie went out for two years in high school. They broke up last year when Jason graduated and came up here for the summer, but of course, when he went home over the winter, they started back up again.

After the first verse is done, I lift the harmonica to my lips, that metallic tang sharp on my tongue. I wheeze along with him, not because I in any way want to encourage the idea of Jason going back to Janie and suburbia, but because if he's in it that deep, even though those two technically broke up again at the beginning of the summer, then I'm down there with him.

He isn't alone in this—not in anything. We laugh together and sweat side by side on the fire line, sure. But we always take our hits together, too—bear any pain across both our shoulders. That's just how it is.

Keep informed of fire weather
conditions and forecasts.

Standard Firefighting Orders, No. 1

CHAPTER 7

I WAS WRONG about not seeing any heat on this fire—after a week of grunt work, the wind shifts again, sending a wall of flames roaring toward us. We feel the wind turn, see the sky change color and the air grow thick with ash. I check over my shoulder every now and then, nervous energy beginning to build. That fire is coming our way—I can feel it out there. But we can't see it yet—*that* stands every hair on my body straight up. Pete's radio scratches and beeps all morning long as crews are pulled off the other flank of the fire and shifted around to our side.

Winds are coming out of the southwest at ten to fifteen miles per hour. Relative humidity is 7 percent. Montana had a wet-enough winter, but with a flash drought hitting the state in the late spring, everything is ready to go up—all it needs is a spark. The mood on our crew turns sober. We just keep cutting line, our muscles complaining as we speed up, even though we've been working hard and fast already.

"Maybe now the rooks in that contract crew behind us will shut up." Jason wipes his forehead, glancing back down the line.

I snort—a mistake in these smoky conditions. I hack and cough while Jason slaps me between the shoulder blades, laughing.

The worst thing about the newbies is they want to see the big fires but don't think twice about walking away from mud so hot it boils if you spray it with water. They think just because they can't see the roots smoldering, they don't need to dig in there and check to be certain that the fire has gone cold. It's the kind of lesson you only need to learn once: that fast is the enemy of good, and that lazy, when it comes to forest fires, puts everybody in danger.

"When that fire rolls across the meadow, it's going to scare the piss out of them."

"Uh-huh."

We get back to work, me still coughing and Jason still laughing at my own rookie mistake. Breaks are down to next to nothing. Rather than reaching for anything time-consuming, like jerky or trail mix, I go straight for one of those goo packets triathletes suck on all the time. It's chalky, nasty stuff that leaves the worst aftertaste. But when you don't have time for anything else and you're burning through calories faster than you can get them down, it's the only thing you want in your pack.

I hand one to Jason when the buzz of Wolf's chainsaw cuts out.

"Keep it. You might need it later."

"Jason. I'm *fine*."

"Yeah, well, let's keep it that way." He fishes a fresh canteen out of my pack and slaps it into my hands.

I take a long drink, stow the leftovers, then check the read-out on my smartwatch. All good, so far. I palm my compass and remind myself of the weather conditions that came in over the radio thirty minutes ago. Above us, the blue sky has turned gray, and the tops of the trees are disappearing. I velcro the shroud over my face. Every so often, the drone of a plane or the whirring blades of a helicopter sounds overhead; they drop lines of retardant to keep the crown from lighting up, or dump bucketloads of water directly on the flames.

When the sky turns an ashy yellow, that chemical fire begins licking up the sides of my legs and ribs, clear to my neck. When you're in the thick of it, smoke blurs the landmarks all around, and it can be hard to tell which way is up. I squint in the direction of our exits. Besides the road we're supposed to drive out on in one direction or the other, we have two other options: there's a decent-sized creek a half mile north or the charred circles of last week's burn piles. And there's the safety zone, of course.

As an absolute last resort, every wildland firefighter carries a fireproof shelter to draw over themselves in case of a burnover if the fire overtakes your position. You scrape down to mineral soil, then pull that shelter over your body and grit your teeth while the fire rolls over you—like offering yourself up as a human Jiffy Pop over a campfire.

That is not an option I plan to take. Ever.

Jason taps my shoulder, then points to the tree line a hundred yards away. Here it comes. The clouds are bright and flickering orange, reflecting the flames below. His face hardens, sharpening with intensity. The bigger the fire and the closer the danger, the quieter Jason becomes.

"Yeah. It's a beast."

We've been working hard all day, but now, with the heat of those flames cresting over us like waves, I'm dripping with sweat. My energy starts to dip.

"Drink up," Pete hollers.

He studies the fire crawling toward us. The flames are getting pretty tall, snapping and hissing upward. We can all feel it—the heat rolling off that flank. It draws the water out of the air. It reaches down your throat and sucks the water out of your mouth, out of your belly, out of every pore in your skin. I fish for my canteen and take it down. Beside me, Jason does the same. We're both breathing hard with exertion and anticipation—and for me at least, the kind of excitement that only lives right on the edge of fear.

Pete reaches for his radio. "I'm calling in a drop. If it isn't here in ten minutes, we're pulling out."

"Roger that." Wolf smacks his hardhat.

"Keep close, stay alert, and be ready to leave all this behind at my signal."

"Okay." He doesn't have to convince me.

I've got my own criteria for when to back off a fire. It comes down to three things: flame height, noise, and heat. I know the fire science people have more precise measures, but out there, on the line, my gut says to pay attention to those three. And right now, all three are firing: flames reaching for the canopy, gusting, oppressive heat, and that wildfire building to a furious roar.

I live for this shit.

I stow my Pulaski and swamp shoulder to shoulder with Jason, chucking the rest of the debris that the sawyers cut well clear of the line. When Pete's radio crackles again, I jump like a jackrabbit. Jason smacks my shoulder with a laugh, but it's a shaky one at best. Nerves are getting the better of us both.

"Clear the line!"

We back away, beneath the cover of high evergreen boughs and the blessed shade they offer. I reach into Jason's pack and fish out a canteen, then he does the same for me—we're both getting low. We stand together, chests heaving, eyes on the sky. We hear the buzz first, then see the plane flying low overhead, against an orange sky. I watch, holding my breath until the slurry slaps against the ground. A dose of that bright red stuff won't stop the fire outright, but if it can keep the treetops from catching fire, the blaze burns with less ferocity. A few more passes cools the area for a while so we can get in there and remove some fuel. It's a limited window, but it gives us ground crews a fighting chance.

"That'll do 'er," Wolf announces.

Pete grimaces. "Breathing room—a little, anyway. Good work, everybody. Let's get in there and knock down what we can, then keep moving down the line."

We work right up until our shift is over. The fire isn't anywhere near contained—a monster like that won't be for a while yet. But I'm pretty damn proud of this crew. We held that fire back through the witching hour—the hottest, windiest part of the day—and that is no small thing.

Fireworks are a particularly bad idea in a state like California, poised as it is to go up in flames at any moment. But somebody always seems to get ahold of the illegal kind over one border or another and the whole world pays the cost.

Like clockwork, a big fire starts north of Tahoe over the holiday weekend. In a snap, the blaze burns clear through the Mt. Shasta wilderness. A week later, it crosses the Oregon border, running up the Cascades.

Hotshots and jumpers from all over the northwest are deployed south. Firefighters from Australia fly in to help, coming to do what they can in their off-season. With so many resources deployed out of state right when the summer thunderstorms begin brewing, there's no hope of covering every lightning strike.

Then the rumors start. A big blowup. An "incident"—which everybody knows means fatalities.

CHAPTER 8

ORDERS COME IN, pulling us off the Yellowstone fire and sending us back to our hotshot compound. Shortly after we arrive, Vick steps into the bed of a mint-green USFS truck, bullhorn in hand. His voice crackles through the speaker, any emotion he may feel broken by the static and hidden behind a pair of mirrored sunglasses.

"At fourteen hundred hours yesterday, a handcrew out of northern Idaho got caught between two walls of fire. We haven't had a burnover situation in—well, it's been a long time. There are no survivors. Members of the shot crew deployed to help clear an exit path sustained serious injuries that will ground some of them for the season."

I swallow, hard. My body might fail me out there where I'll be too far from a hospital to recover—I know that. But dying on a fire because all the watch-outs and orders, the radios and weather updates, all the safety measures still aren't enough—that's another thing entirely. I don't want to die engulfed in flames I can't escape. None of us does.

The bullhorn screeches as Vick's trigger finger goes slack. He lets the thing drop to his hip, then raises it again a time or two before he's able to speak again. "I don't have to tell you that what happened yesterday changes things. Every loss to a wildland crew is a loss for all of us. Thanks to rising temperatures and forests packed full of fuel, fire behavior is changing—we're doing what we can to stay ahead of it. You can be sure, in the months and years that follow, we will study what happened out there so we never get caught in that situation again.

"We are being retasked to the Red Rock fire that just broke out. That fire doesn't care if we're in mourning. It's still burning, and we have to go meet it. That's our job." Vick clears his throat. "You already know recruitment for wildland fire is down across the board and has been for a few seasons now. We haven't been able to fill vacancies with qualified applicants, never mind how this incident will set our numbers back.

"Admin is putting folks who'd normally have a cushy desk job in the Forest Service, or fieldwork in fisheries or wildlife man-agement at the Bureau of Land Management, through a week of standard fire camp, starting tomorrow. That personnel will slot into handcrews; those firefighters will shift to fill your posts as needed, freeing you all up to fill other vacancies requiring initial-attack experience. Now, while this may be your second or third season on a shot crew, and under normal circumstances you wouldn't move to a permanent posting or leadership position for another few years, we're going to need you to step up. I'll be calling several of you in over the next few days with new postings."

Vick clicks off the mic.

My heart rate ticks up. Nerves crackle and spike through our crew like lightning between thunderheads. And beneath that, a ground current of fear. Eager as any of us are to get after that next fire, coming face-to-face with the life and death reality of the work we do is—well, it's hard.

But chances to jump the line don't come along often. Okay, never. The kind of quick promotion Vick's talking about is unheard of. Jason scuffs his feet in the gravel—I don't have to look up to know there's a grimace creasing his face. To his way of thinking, I'm always too eager, too ready to leap ahead of myself, too willing to reach too far for my own good. And he isn't wrong.

But it isn't disapproval, not really—it's fear. He's scared for me. For what I might do to prove to everybody that I'm capable of something I'm nowhere near ready for.

Everybody's always been worried about me, constantly. And with good reason, I guess.

I was a sick kid. I don't remember Valentine's Day parties

or water balloon fights at Field Day or any of the rest of that fun stuff from elementary school. I remember tubes down my throat, needles scarring my arms, and a million beeping, burping machines. Those exam rooms have a particular smell—obnoxious sterility. Industrial-strength disappointment. Clinical doom. To this day, I have to talk myself down from puking every time I go into one.

My parents and I were in and out of a gajillion doctors' offices, but we never left with any answers. It made my mom crazy—this puzzle she couldn't solve. This thing that was hurting me that she couldn't fix.

Then, for some reason the doctors could never explain, whatever it was just stopped by the time I turned twelve. My body became strong again. Really strong. So when, a few years later, in the middle of junior year, I started dropping weight no matter how much I ate and struggled through bouts of dizziness and confusion, it was back to the domino line of doctors. Another battery of tests. Full-body scans, test chambers, blood draws, my veins scarred and withered and every bit as stubborn as I am. Another wave of sleepless nights, my parents pacing the hall outside my bedroom.

But this time, the doctors had an answer.

My parents sat, stunned, on one side of the exam table, while Jason sat on the other, with me in between, desperate to hear anything other than the fact that my body had betrayed me again. The endocrinologist explained that type 1 diabetes is a condition I'll have for the rest of my life. He cheerily offered that it was perfectly manageable with careful monitoring and insulin dosages, assuming I didn't overexert myself with strenuous physical activities that could deplete my already taxed systems.

Right.

By seventeen, I was already hell-bent on a career in wildland firefighting. And I knew I wanted to push myself until I earned a spot jumping out of planes to get to those fires.

I'd already been held back once; I wasn't going to let that happen again.

Then, I think to scare me, he mentioned that monitoring diabetes was an around-the-clock job, that low blood sugar was as dangerous as high blood sugar, and that I could slip into a diabetic coma in the middle of the night and never wake up. Well, that decided it for me. If I had to pick between dying in my sleep or out on the fire line, I knew my choice. Didn't have to think twice about it.

The doctor rattled off a series of symptoms and risk factors, but all I could process was the fact that no way would any crew boss pick me over the other dozen badass candidates who weren't a health risk and a liability. So I decided right there, in that crepey exam gown, with my insides and my outsides on display for everyone to see and weigh in on, that I'd have to keep the diagnosis a secret.

I think my insistence on fire no matter the risks is what broke things between me and my parents—they were on the home stretch, had kept this sickly child alive all those years. And then, when I was almost out of the house and out of their care, safe and sound, something else went wrong. And rather than take the treatment advice the medical professionals recommended, and accept the long list of things I couldn't or shouldn't do, I threw myself headlong into a line of work that was probably going to get me killed.

At least, that's what they saw.

But by the time fire season started after my junior year, I was eighteen and able to make my own medical decisions.

Aunt Cate knew better than to try to talk me out of it. Instead, she made it her job to help me track my insulin levels at various exertion and hydration scenarios, and to use sports gummies packed with electrolytes and known quantities of carbohydrates to help prevent a dangerous event out on a fire. And she modified my tech, too, so I could enter my carb intake on a smartwatch instead of at the insulin pump jabbed into my abdomen, meaning I could discreetly track my numbers while I was in the field, surrounded by other firefighters. Every diabetic is different; it took some time to figure out what kinds of carbs, in what quantities, kept my glucose level steady in high-stress, high-activity situations.

And it worked—only Jason knows the truth.

I made him promise to help me hide it on the job. But sometimes I wonder if Jason would've taken that football scholarship if he weren't so committed to keeping me out of the ER. Sometimes I wonder if he'd be out here at all if it weren't for me and my condition. Some nights, when I'm staring up at a smoky, starless sky, I wonder if I had any right to ask that of him in the first place.

Anatomy of a Wildfire

finger: A bulge protruding from the main fire, at times
    moving in a different direction and speed.

flank: A side of the fire, tending to spread outward to
    consume fuel if left uncontained.

head: The advancing front of the fire, usually containing the
    highest flame height, intensity, and rate of spread.

heel: The rear of the fire, already burnt black; usually where
    the fire began.

spot: Embers or other flammable material flung beyond
    the borders of the main fire; handcrews "grid the
    green" to search for spot fires to prevent the outbreak
    of multiple fires.

CHAPTER 9

WHILE WE WAIT for our turn with Vick, Jason and I are put on abatement, supervising a contract crew clearing a stand of dead pine trees killed by invasive beetles. It's a long, hot day, with a relative humidity low enough to put everybody on edge. This late in the season, controlled burns are out of the question, but chainsaws spark and there are plenty of idiots who don't think twice about a stray cigarette butt left smoking.

When we finally get back to camp, I am as tired from standing around doing nothing but fighting my own nerves as I would have been constructing line all day. Vick waves from outside the office, hollering for me and Jason to get over there, so we drop our gear and duck inside. Nobody's ever *really* clean on the compound, but our faces are smeared with a paste of sweat and sawdust. And we stink.

Vick tucks his thumbs in his belt loops, puffing out his chest. He looks at Jason and me sidelong, shaking his head a little. "Can't believe I'm saying this to a pair of second-year temps: I got a call from Missoula and apparently they're fast-tracking another round of rookie smokejumper training, pulling exclusively from crew already working at the elite level who had previously applied."

He pulls his lower lip through his teeth. The man can hardly bring himself to speak the words.

I stiffen, clamp my mouth shut, and fix my eyes on the floor. Is he saying what I think he's saying?

"If you ask me, both of you could use another ten years on the fire line before you even think about jumping out of planes. And you"—he levels his finger at me while I try not to wince—"need to cool your heels. You need to be patient—take the time to learn from the senior firefighters on this crew who still have a thing or two to teach you, whether you want to believe that or not."

Vick shuffles a stack of papers on his desk. "But without reopening the application process, and eliminating firefighters in essential leadership positions, it seems you two made the cut. Jason, your time on the engine crew that was dispatched to the Wild Basin fire in Colorado last fall impressed them. And Blair, your backcountry skills and one hell of a recommendation from the volunteer coordinator up in Trout Creek convinced them—no matter what I said about the pair of you being too green, and you, Blair, far too reckless.

"Now, Jason, you've got a decision to make. You can go to

smokejumper training if that's what you want. But you've also got an offer for a spot on a helitack crew out of Idaho."

My mouth goes dry. I don't look at Jason—I can't, though his eyes bear down on me with the kind of intensity even a stump could feel. A helitack stint is a great opportunity—he'd be a member of the crew right away, with no training to wash out of. He'd learn how to scout fires from the air, how to rappel safely out of a helicopter, and maybe most important, how to find his place on a different kind of crew. A few years there would give Jason the kind of experience that would land him at the top of the candidate list for smokejumpers in a normal year—and the confidence to know he belonged.

He should take it. No question.

But—I'm going to jumper training, no matter what. I just don't want to do it without him.

"I'm grateful for the opportunity, but Blair and I are a team."

Vick stares for a long moment, eyes flicking between the two of us, to be sure we understand in no uncertain terms just how unfavorably he views this decision. "Get cleaned up—you reek. And pack your things. I have a fresh batch of rookies to whip into shape who'll be needing your beds this evening. You both are due at the Missoula smokejumper base first thing tomorrow morning."

Seriously?

He hands over our transfer papers. "That's it."

This is seriously happening?

"Um, thanks," Jason says as we back away.

I dart outside, letting the door bang shut behind me. I can't hold it in a second longer—I shriek, chucking my hardhat in the air. It lands like an upside-down turtle, spinning. Jason grabs me around the waist, hefts me up, and whirls us both in a dizzy circle. When he sets me back down on the ground, he's out of breath and grinning like an idiot.

"Can you believe it?'

"I *told* you we'd get in."

He throws his head back and laughs. "You said if we applied every year for a decade, we'd wear them down eventually. Nobody said we'd get in halfway through our second year on the job."

I can't argue with that. "My time on that contract crew must have counted toward the minimum, or maybe even all those volunteer hours?"

Jason blanches. "I, uh, gotta call my mom. I swore up and down this wouldn't actually happen for years. And Janie. *Shit*."

I cackle, backing away as he runs for the barracks. I'm not paying attention to where I'm going, stumbling around in a daze, when Vick's voice floats through the open window at the back of the offices.

"They'll be there tomorrow morning." A long pause follows. "You're telling me. Teenagers have no business jumping out of planes. They'll wash out by the end of hell week; send them right back here, where they'll be my problem again."

I back away, quickly. Of course Vick would think we'll never make it. But do the people in Missoula feel that way, too? Suddenly, my excitement seems foolish. Am I just a box they can check off? Wash out the kids so you can make it look like you started with a respectable candidate pool?

No. I have more going for me than anyone can read on an application. I've been training for this moment for years. I only ran cross-country because I read that every morning at smoke-jumper training begins with a distance run. Sophomore year I stole two twenty-pound discs from the weight room and lugged them around in my backpack every day to get used to hauling ridiculously heavy packs. And last season, whenever Pete got called away to deal with admin crap right when we got off a fire, I offered to clean and sharpen his saw. Every time an engine crew called for support, I volunteered so I could learn as much as possible about the hoses, fittings, and pumps. I made damn sure I was capable of handling at least twice as much as my job description claimed.

Nah—there's no way I'll fail even one of their tests. This isn't the first time somebody has underestimated me, and it won't be the last. If they aren't ready to give everyone a fair shot, I'll just have to take mine.

In the northernmost reaches of the state, a sparking bundle of pine needles is flung from treetop to treetop, the fire tossed over a wide river that should have stopped it in its tracks. Thirty minutes later, that spark becomes a blaze of its own. Sixty minutes later, a lookout calls it in. And twenty minutes after that, a fixed-wing aircraft circles over the building fire, dropping its load of jumpers over the forest.

Two at a time, they fall through the air, buoyed by their chutes and steering into a steep alpine meadow. The plane banks one last time, drops boxes of gear, and then heads for home. Before the drone of the engine fades, the jumpers have melted into the trees. And by the time the sun eases out of sight, the fire is gone.

CHAPTER 10

JASON AND I stop by Aunt Cate's on the way to Missoula—well, if you can call Aunt Cate's *on the way* to anything. When we arrive, Jason swings out of the pickup and lifts her off her feet a good eighteen inches. They're both laughing when he sets her back down again. I sling an arm over their shoulders and Aunt Cate squeezes back while we cross the patio to the house.

Jason makes himself comfortable by the outdoor grill, plucking away at his ukulele while Aunt Cate preps elk steaks from last fall's hunt. I crack a fizzy water for myself, a root beer for Jason, and a bottle of the local IPA that Aunt Cate buys by the case. We clink our drinks and I settle beside Jason, my boot propped against the side of his chair.

"So tell me again, one more time, how exactly a pair of sophomore temporary hires made it into smokejumper training?"

I sputter, "Anybody with initial-attack experience was considered for this second round—hotshots, helitack crews—"

"*Riiiiight,* right." Aunt Cate nods while she generously salts the steaks.

Jason laughs, tipping his head back.

I smack his arm. "Remember, Jason's halfway through his associate's in fire science. And I served all those summers on the volunteer fire crew *and* camp crews—and don't forget that contract crew."

Jason snorts. "They're desperate. It's the only explanation."

"Speak for yourself." I may be young, but I deserve this, no matter what anybody thinks.

Aunt Cate watches us with a bemused smile. "I have no doubt the pair of you will be some of the best smokejumpers to ever come out of the Missoula base. I just wish you had a little more experience under your belt."

"We'll be all right, Aunt Cate," Jason says.

She sighs, flips the steaks, and comes to sit on the wooden arm of my Adirondack. "Well, I can't say I've exactly followed the rules in my career either. But promise me one thing—"

"Yeah?" I wait for what I know is coming.

"Blair, the exertion level—"

"I can handle it."

She bites her lower lip. "I'm sure you can. But jumpers work in really remote places. If your blood sugar spikes in the middle of nowhere . . ."

"I'll be *fine*. You know I've wanted this for longer than—"

"I know." She lets out a slow breath. "But wanting something and being ready for it are not the same."

"I *am* ready." *Now* Aunt Cate is second-guessing me? She's always been supportive—I don't get it.

"Just promise me, if you get in over your head, you'll walk away. There is no shame in regrouping, and then trying again when you're a little older."

She's speaking to both of us, but her eyes are fixed on me.

"Promise," Jason says, still plucking away.

"Blair?"

"Yes, Aunt Cate. I promise."

All through dinner, Aunt Cate tries to make small talk about the smoky morning sunrises or the ash landing in the rivers and warming things too much to allow for any fly-fishing. But I hardly listen—my head is already miles away.

When we say our goodbyes, Aunt Cate holds on a little longer than she normally would.

"Don't worry," I say.

She pinches her lips together. "I'll try. So long as you don't give me any reason to."

We pull into the base, a modest clump of buildings situated west of the Missoula airport. If it weren't for the enormous Forest Service logo on the side of the loft, it could be another hangar for private pilot lessons or rich people flying in on the way to their swanky ranches outside Helena or bordering the national park. The lot is full of Subarus and four-wheel-drive trucks with a few RVs parked at the far end—pretty much what you'd expect from people who work in the wilderness. The minute they get some time off work, they head back into the wilderness to play there, too.

We step out of the truck, Jason moaning and stretching, and me trying to tamp down the excitement that has my insides fizzling and popping clear to my toes. I've flown over these buildings dozens of times, dreaming of the day when I'd belong here.

Admin directs us to the dormitory alongside the training center. The buildings all have the same orange overhanging roofs, with an old-school Smokey Bear vibe about the place. Carefully manicured flower bushes hug the borders of the stolid buildings, the walkways swept clean of debris. I spot a dozen or so smokejumpers around the base—they all look to be in their thirties and forties. And they aren't shy about watching the new crop of rookies arrive, making it plenty clear they don't expect any of us to last.

I'm sent to one end of the dorm, while Jason is directed to the other, where all the guys are chatting, slapping backs, shaking hands, and sizing one another up. At all the other camps I've been in, there were a handful of other women—depending on the base's size, sometimes two or three, sometimes a dozen. But here, so far all I see is me.

I take a minute, gather my breath. I have Jason. I don't need anyone else. But it's exhausting always being different—lonely in a way that nibbles at the edges of my resolve. I dump my bags in my room and close the door. I shake my head to snap myself out of it. I have other things to worry about.

At the bottom of my gear bag, inside a locked box, I keep a spare transmitter with enough extra sensors to last for months, along with a glucometer and a stockpile of long-acting and rapid-acting insulin. I peel down my underwear, pull off the old sensor, jab a new one into my abdomen, close to my hip bone, then click the transmitter into place. It's low-profile enough that nobody can see it through my clothing unless I wear something super formfitting, which is highly unlikely.

I tap through to the app on my smartwatch and wait for the readings to come in. As long as everything works properly, and as long as I punch in the grams of carbs in anything I eat, my pump will keep my glucose level steady. Sure, I have to eat like a horse, keep my carb intake low and consistent, carefully manage my stress levels, and stay hydrated. But I'm lucky—this tech wasn't available even a few years ago. And not everybody has an Aunt Cate handy to tailor it all to their specific needs.

Aunt Cate fixed the pump so it won't beep or hiss to alert

anyone that there is anything about me that needs medical monitoring. As long as the insulin pump and sensor are attached, and the transmitter is working, my watch will only pulse when something needs my attention—if my blood sugar dips too low or rises too high. So I have a fancy watch—whatever. Lots of people do, these days. If anybody gives me shit about it, I have a ready excuse about GPS and weather data to shut them up.

Over the winter, Aunt Cate helped me test a system where I monitored my levels without the pump, used a glucometer to test my levels, and injected myself regularly with insulin. We did it all in town, with an ER and endocrinologist nearby if we needed them. Then we repeated the whole process under the strain of sustained, intense exercise—long hikes in heavy packs, and conditioning circuits in the heat of the day—adding a regimen of energy gels and gummies to the mix, and still my numbers held. It was a pain in the ass to stick myself all the time and take all those manual readings, but it was reassuring to know that I could handle it if, for some reason, all my tech failed out in the field. Anyway, Aunt Cate insisted—she was ready to reveal my condition to my supervisors if I couldn't manage that backup system. Then she taught Jason how to watch for signs that my blood sugar was too low or too high so if disorientation or shock kicked in, he knew what to do.

It's a lot, and I didn't ask for any of this. Jason didn't ask for a full-time job as a second set of eyes and half-trained emergency medic either. But I'm not going to waste time feeling sorry for myself. And I'm definitely not going to let it hold me, or Jason, back.

I shove the locked box into the back of my closet, then head outside to poke around the base a little on my own. First stop: the runway, where the planes wait to transport loads of jumpers into the middle of nowhere. I walk through open doors into the ready room filled with row after row of lockers packed with gear and a big yellow sign that says STUPID HURTS. Next door is the packing room, with long tables down the center for round chutes and another set of angled ones for squares. Sewing machines line the wall, with antler racks and elk mounts filling the space between windows.

I peek into another room with still more sewing machines—there must be dozens of them. With nobody around to stop me, I wander into the loft and tower, where I turn in a slow circle, looking up. The ceiling is at least twice as high as the other buildings, numbered in a grid with ropes hanging down. A few chutes are clipped in and dangling, ready for inspection. The translucent fabric catches the light, softening it where it falls.

I wander back outside, skirting Operations and its steady hum of activity. Instead, I follow a dirt track leading west—probably the beginning of the two-mile running circuit I've read about. I don't get far before a series of steel towers come into view. Two are white, one sort of like inverted football uprights, the other one like something you might find on a ropes course. Drawing closer, I can make out a series of wires strung between them, dropping at a sharp angle toward the ground; it's sort of a cross between a zip line and a ski lift. Parachute trails hang limp, ready for a jumper-in-training to clip in.

That'll be me soon.

The thought hits my stomach like a brick. I did everything I could think of to prepare for this—push-ups, sit-ups, pull-ups, distance runs, and punishing hikes. Why didn't I ever think to work climbing into that rotation? Even some basic rappelling would have helped. Harnesses and ropes and hanging, static, in the air will all be new to me, and I'll have to figure that shit out under pressure.

Even though it's eighty degrees outside, a cold sweat breaks out on my upper lip. It doesn't make any sense—bridge jumping and cliff diving don't rattle me at all, and I can't wait to be in the rear door of one of those aircraft. I *really* can't wait to hurl myself out that door and into the waiting sky. But the idea of hanging from a bunch of cables just high enough to break a person into bits if they fall—

I swallow, hard, and look away.

Beside the white towers is a broad orange one with stairs

leading all the way up to what looks like a vintage VW bus propped three stories up in the air. I glance back over my shoulder. I shouldn't go up there—it's surely off-limits. But nobody is around to see.

I cross under the shadow of the broad metal body and take the steps up two at a time. When my head pops through the opening in the floor, the bus-like cabin suddenly makes sense—the cutout windows are exactly where they would be in an aircraft, with the open door at the rear, and cables running to the opposite towers. So this is where we'll practice jumping?

I let out a long breath, cross to the doorway, and sit, letting my feet dangle in the open air. I wait while the sky dims and insects in the field below pipe up, welcoming dusk. I stay put, acquainting myself with the height and the ground far below, until the brick in my stomach and the cold sweats are gone, and at least in my head, I'm ready for whatever the instructors might throw at me.

In the arid southwest, grass fires rip across the land, burning hot and fast. In the humid southeast, regular fires sweep through the forests and lick them clean, keeping the loblolly pines from taking over the native shortleaf's habitat. In the far north, desiccated landscapes erupt in massive peat fires, burning down and out, carving giant holes into the soil.

Every region has its particular challenge, but in the mountainous West, it's the vast stretches of wilderness—the very reason people are drawn there—that makes the region's forests downright indefensible. By the time you shuttle your crews out to the nearest road, and then hike those crews overland, the fire has spread beyond the point of containment. Unless, that is, you can find a way to drop a team of highly trained wildland firefighters into the middle of that wilderness.

For that, you need smokejumpers.

CHAPTER 11

WHY ANYONE WOULD bother applying if they can't manage the basic fitness test is beyond me—I've been doing double this circuit of seven dead-hang pull-ups, forty-five sit-ups, twenty-five push-ups, and a mile-and-a-half run in under eleven minutes as my warm-up for at least a year.

I sit in the thirsty dirt of the training field while the last few recruits sweat and grunt through the fitness test. The sun overhead is muted by a low layer of clouds, but it still manages to glare down at us. An intermittent wind whips up little dust devils around our running shoes, mixing with the sweat dripping off our skin.

Jason hunkers down beside me while we wait for the last few recruits to finish. "Those idiots are in for a real surprise when they find out the three-mile pack hike isn't on flat ground as advertised."

"Yeah." Idiots.

Whining aside, everybody passes the PT test.

When the base manager steps up to speak, I hop up, jamming my hands into my pockets to keep myself from fidgeting. He's lanky for a smokejumper, probably at the upper end of the height limit. What hair he has left is steely gray, and his face has the weathered look of someone who's spent his life outdoors.

"My name is William Hawkins and I am the Region One manager. We had already selected our jumpers for the year in our training this past spring; a half dozen people from that class of elite firefighters with ten times your experience washed out." He loops his thumbs through the belt cinched at his hips. "I want to be clear about one thing: none of you are supposed to be here."

I bite down so not even a flicker of disappointment shows. He's just putting on a show, right? They wouldn't bring us all here just to cut us—admin wouldn't even bother with a second round of training if they didn't need reinforcements. At least, I'm doing my best to convince myself of that fact.

"We normally experience a thirty-three percent washout rate when candidates have had all spring to prepare physically for the rigors of rookie training. You may feel prepared for fire season on your old crew, but this is another level."

He scans the assembled candidates, tipping his sunglasses down.

"This time around, we anticipate doubling that washout number, just so you know where you stand."

Heels dig in, toes scuff the dirt, apprehension rises like the puffs of dust around our ankles. Beside me, Jason juts out his chin. Yeah, they told us we'd never make the cut for our hotshot crew last year. Underestimating the two of us just because we're young—that's a mistake. A ripple of excitement catches me like a shiver. Let's go already.

"There will be classroom sessions, practice jumps, and hours of meticulous preparation so that before you ever jump on a fire, your muscles know what to do even if your brain quits on you. If you thought you knew all about tending your gear when you were on an engine crew or loading into a helicopter, you've got another thing coming. There is nothing—and I mean nothing—like the single-minded focus you will need to care for the gear that is the only thing preventing you from plummeting to the earth."

Without any more fanfare, Hawkins turns his back, returning to Operations. Uneasy muttering fills in the space he left behind.

"That's it?" Jason whispers.

"Doubt it." I look over my shoulder; a guy with a USFS ball cap pulled over shaggy blond hair holds a clipboard across his chest, watching us. I jab Jason in the ribs and turn around. Once the rest of the recruits do the same, the guy with the clipboard speaks up.

"You can call me Griggs. I'll be your primary trainer—under normal circumstances there'd be more of us, but this is not a normal fire season, as you all know." He turns on his heel, talking over his shoulder while he makes for the base. "Find the set of gear with your name on it; stand in front of the pile and await further instructions."

He walks at a fast clip, and we hustle to keep up. In the ready room, my name is taped across the top of an empty cubby with a clean set of Nomex inside and a jumpsuit draped outside. The place smells like a high school locker room—stale sweat and weathered gear. Plus that woodsy scent of a wildland station, mixed with chainsaw oil and gasoline.

I've never seen a jumpsuit up close before. I run a finger along the stiff material and bite down on my lip to keep the thrill from showing all over my face.

Griggs pulls on one piece of gear after another, calling out instructions. "Nomex makes up the base layer; don't forget your ankle braces." He leans over to zip the legs all the way up. "Your jumpsuit is made out of Kevlar to protect you from a bad fall or a tree landing—it's so thick that we cut it with a saw to make repairs. It's also fireproof in case something goes very wrong up there and you drop *into* the fire instead of near it."

A few nervous chuckles scatter through the air, but Griggs is clearly not joking.

He twists around so we can see the padding stitched into the jacket. "The suit is full of pockets and storage compartments—I like to pack my tent so it's flush against my lower back where I could use a little extra cushion. The poles go in a pocket at my shin, along with some extra clothes and ropes in case I land in a tree, or in case the gear box does."

One by one, the guys begin stripping down and stepping into their jumpsuits. I learned in my first wildland season to always wear a base layer I wouldn't be shy about the whole world seeing me in, one that wouldn't reveal the shape of the sensor, pump, and transmitter stuck to my abdomen, if I was quick enough about changing. So before anybody can make a crack about my needing special accommodations, I drop my pants and step into the forest-green ones in my cubby. They're a little stiff, and I'll sub them out for ones that won't chafe as soon as Griggs gives us a break, but they'll do for now. I button up the yellow shirt, flexing and straightening my arms to check the length of the cuffs. Next, Jason and I take turns helping each other into our jumpsuits. I hike the suspenders over my shoulders, then shrug into the jacket with thick black straps and hooks stitched over the top. The thing is heavy! I've never been small, and I wouldn't want to be, but that marshmallow suit makes me twice as wide all the way around. We all practice helping each other in and out of our suits a few times before Griggs calls a halt and we hang them up.

Next, he takes us on a tour of the gear room for the most comprehensive lesson in sewing I've ever received. "We check the chutes after every jump, and we repair them ourselves. When you are up there falling through the sky with nothing but the work of your hands or your buddy's hands keeping you aloft, you'll be glad you triple-checked every seam."

Okay, so maybe I was expecting some razzing about sewing and me being the only female in sight, but Griggs's no-nonsense approach doesn't leave any room for that shit. He plunks himself down at the machine and sets about his instructions. Heat, like from those chemical flames that always lick over my skin before I head out on a fire, begins to burn low in my belly. Adrenaline. Cortisol. Dopamine. And insulin, of course.

Maybe, *just maybe*, I'll get the same shot in this place as everybody else.

Fire Watch-Out Situations

No. 4: Unfamiliar with weather and local factors influencing fire behavior.

CHAPTER 12

AFTER LUNCH, JASON balls up the remnants of his sack lunch and tosses it into the trash can, flicking his fingers, that flop-wrist follow-through second nature even though there's no ball or court for miles. "Is that all? We can't be done for the day already."

I stuff the last two bites of a banana smeared with peanut butter into my cheek like a squirrel storing up for winter. "No way."

Jason got the scoop on the other candidates last night: A dozen are in their twenties and thirties and have worked in fire for at least a decade. Some have engine experience, some have been crew bosses, and a few have even worked on helitack or rappeller crews. That leaves another six with half that experience. Then there are a handful of teenagers—every one of them Eagle Scouts or all-star athletes or something.

Jason stretches high, then leans in with a smirk. "You're already tallying who's going to wash out in the first week, aren't you?"

"Uh-huh."

"You're ruthless, Blair."

I chuckle, dipping my head to roll out my neck. "Well it's not going to be us. So who *is* it going to be?"

"All right. I'll play." Jason scans the group. He pauses on a lanky redhead whose gaze never seems to settle on anything. "Him."

"Yeah? Why?"

"He's never going to be able to bank enough calories to keep up."

I nod slowly. "You're probably right."

"Your turn."

I drop my gaze, then glance around, chewing on the corner of my lip, wondering how many of them have me pegged as the first to drop. "That guy in the teal ball cap."

"Really? He's jacked."

"Yeah, but this training is as much about mental toughness as physical. And—I don't know—he looks spooked."

Jason sits back, his eyes going wide.

"Come on—I wasn't talking about you," I rush to add. "You've got this. You'll probably top the whole class."

Before I have the chance to see if my reassurance lands, Griggs rounds the corner, hands on hips. "Suit up! Packs, hardhats, Pulaskis, and supplies for an overnight shift."

I shoot out of my seat. A couple of guys groan, but they

move quickly enough. We load into trucks and are driven off base, into the Forest Service roads near Blue Mountain. When the trucks park in an unmarked pullout, we tumble out again, threading supply boxes through the handles of our tools, ready for a long hike.

Jason falls in beside me. "Twenty-four hours, right off the bat?"

I flash a smile. "What else would you expect?"

Griggs takes off at a steady pace and we hustle to form two lines behind him. Aunt Cate taught me young not to tuck my chin, looking at my boots for a long hike. Sure, watching where you put your feet is important, but if you cut off your airway, every step is going to be a struggle. So while we begin the climb, I keep my chin high and my shoulders down, my eyes fixed on the clouds. I'm glad for the shade under those tall trees and a little birdsong—I'm excited, and trying hard to convince myself I'm not also a little terrified. I try to distract myself by thinking up a name for the particular blue of the sky or the jagged shape it carves out between treetops. When we get to the top of the ridge, Griggs stops and drops his pack, and we scatter to fill the space around him.

"You are going to dig a line straight down this ridge. We're looking for people who can work hard and fast. This may not be a live fire, but you will wear your protective gear the entire time. Now spread out—"

We drop the supply boxes at his feet and sift downhill into a single-file line, four feet away from one another. I cinch my gloves and adjust my hip belt for working instead of hiking.

"—and go."

I grab the shaft of my Pulaski, heft it, and sink the blade into the ground, yanking as I bring it back up again, dislodging a chunk of warm, dark soil. I take a shuffling step, then do it again. And again. And again.

Working on a fire line is not for anybody who can't handle repetitive tasks. It is not for someone who doesn't like punishing physical work. Aunt Cate sometimes describes gardening in the raised beds by her back door as active meditation; if you ask me, digging line is like that. You've got one purpose. It's no good worrying about what will happen an hour later or a day later or a month down the line. You clear your mind and you dig. And if you do that for long enough, you dig a line all the way around the perimeter of a fire.

Now, it would be a lot easier to be Zen about the whole thing without Griggs tromping up and down the line, hollering, "Eighteen inches! I want to see nothing but mineral soil." Or, "Tired yet? Wanna quit?"

It's not like we're at football tryouts or in the damn military. Why people think they've got to beat you down when the dirt and the long hours are already doing an excellent job of that is beyond me. So I mostly ignore the yelling, except for when Griggs gets in Jason's face about a root he only severed but didn't chop completely out of the line. Then Griggs hollers at me to pick up my pace, but he must only be looking for something to gripe about, because we haven't really spread out yet; if I go any faster, I'll sink the blade of my Pulaski right into the next guy's hardhat.

I do well for the first four or so hours, stopping regularly for water breaks and to gnaw on a couple of gummies. But as the sun goes down and he keeps us at it, I start to spin a little. There is no fire on the other side of that line. Griggs is only keeping us at it in the name of torture, to test our mental toughness. It's one thing to bust your ass to keep a fire from cresting a ridge and rolling over a mountain town or into a nature preserve. Digging to prove a point? That's annoying as hell. More importantly, it saps your energy if your mind and heart aren't fully committed to what you're putting your body through.

Griggs knows all this, and he's waiting to see who'll give in first.

As darkness descends with no sign of us letting up, I switch on my headlamp. Halfway through the night, somebody pukes behind a tree. We work while the moon rises. We work while the Milky Way Tilt-A-Whirls above. We work while even the forest sleeps.

I made sure I conditioned hard before the season started so I could score at the very top of the fitness tests and work grueling sixteen-hour shifts without lagging, all without big swings in blood sugar. If anybody—on the hotshot crew or here—had any idea I'm hiding a complicated medical condition, I'd be out on my ass. But tonight, all I can think about is how my neck aches and my right shoulder and left lats burn from swinging that damn Pulaski hour after hour. My insulin pump is keeping up, adjusting as my glucose levels dip and rise again. The readout on my smartwatch isn't as steady a line as I'd like, but it'll do.

At three in the morning, Griggs calls a break. Everybody stumbles around to find a stretch of flat ground, and without even discussing the matter, Jason and I lie down back-to-back to share a little heat, wrapping our tarps over our shoulders. We shiver on the forest floor for an hour before Griggs gets us up again and back on the line.

The sun bearing down on my clammy skin as morning dawns is unbearably cruel. My pace grows slower and slower as the morning wears on. I ran out of water and blew through my food after the catnap—that snack was the only way I talked myself up off the ground. Finally, around ten o'clock, after we've been at it for something like fourteen hours, Griggs calls a halt. Sagging in relief, we mostly slide downhill to the truck.

"I need a shower," Jason grumbles.

"Yeah, you do." We're both too exhausted to crack a smile.

I drop my pack, refill my canteens at the truck, then shuck my boots and peel off my disgusting wool socks. We both collapse in the dirt.

"How are your levels?" Jason asks.

With a groan, I lift my watch and tap through the display. "A little low—nothing urgent."

"Bullshit," he groans. "Snacks. Water. Don't make me get up, I'm begging you."

I dig in my pocket and choke down a couple gummies even though they taste like dust. Chewy, sticky dust. Surely the energy it takes to gnaw them into chunks small enough to swallow far outweighs any benefit of actually consuming them. But I do it anyway.

"Drink."

Too exhausted to argue, I tip back my canteen and don't put it down until it's empty. "There. Happy?"

"Ecstatic."

I lean back, soaking in the morning sunlight, eyes closed, already halfway asleep. Griggs drops the tailgate on one of the trucks, the *bang!* snapping me back to attention. I sit up—eighteen pairs of running shoes are lined up in the back, with cotton socks stuffed inside. A shiver of unease ripples through me. There are my runners, and my socks, third from the left, meaning some-body rummaged through my room to find them. All my insulin and spare sensors are in a box at the back of my closet—what if somebody saw those, too? What if they became curious, or worse, suspicious?

A wide grin splits Griggs's face as he sets his clipboard on the tailgate. I'm beginning to hate that damn clipboard.

"Usually, a recruit gets several opportunities to misstep before they fail. But we can't afford that kind of leniency right now. You can't hack the morning runs? Back to the fire line, where you're needed. You can't focus on the book learning? Back to an engine crew, where you can do some good. You can't execute a PLF when you hit the ground? Back to a helitack crew, where the pilots do the landing part for you."

I grit my teeth. Tired as I am, nobody is going to sweet-talk me into leaving.

"There's no shame in failing here—we can only take the best of the best. If that's not you, you're welcome to try again in a few years' time." He nods, and a woman steps around the side of the truck, her hands clasped behind her back so the muscles in her shoulders pop. She's as tall as Griggs and every bit as solid.

"We start most days with a run. Your trainer, Watters here, will put you through your paces."

Watters doesn't say anything, just turns and takes off at a jog down the dirt road. After a few uncertain seconds, Griggs muses, "Well, what are you waiting for?"

"Shit." I scramble to grab my runners, yank them on, and tie the laces, but my hands are cramping into claws and I can barely pull the loops taut.

One of the recruits chucks his runners back into the truck. "Hell no." It's the burly guy I bet against yesterday at lunch—what seems like a million years ago.

Griggs barely raises an eyebrow. "Is there a problem?"

I peek under my arm as I cinch the last knot, throwing a smirk Jason's way.

"Unbelievable," he mutters.

I lurch to my feet and take off down the road after Watters, the sound of the burly guy's shouting and Griggs's calm dismissals fading.

Just like that, eighteen candidates become seventeen.

It doesn't take long for the pack to close in, and despite our fatigue, everybody jostles to get to the front, to prove that they belong. Some of the guys seem too muscle-bound to last long at this pace. Working a chainsaw and running any kind of distance are two very different skill sets, calling for two very different body types. Those guys will have the advantage when it comes to pull-ups and clearing logs out of the sawyer's way. But there is more to this job than muscle.

A handful of us are decent runners. My eyes lock onto Watters's stubby black ponytail twitching at the front of the pack. My feet are screaming at me to stop, but with each stride, the long muscles down my legs seem to loosen and stretch out, and though I'm bone-tired, the run actually feels good. And the fresh pair of socks are a godsend—not that I'll admit that fact to Griggs any-time soon.

Even so, I hold back, not wanting to stress my already pulver-ized muscles or send my blood sugar plummeting. Instead, I focus on my breath. The tension drains out of my shoulders and my fists loosen. My jaw goes slack, and my mind, too. Miles fall away beneath my feet, and without even thinking about it, I slip past the rest of the rookies like a salmon on a ladder, up and over the dam. I pull up a half pace behind Watters and to the left. Our strides sync and everything else falls away.

Watters leads us down an old logging road, along a single-track up the ridge, then gradually downslope through the sparse woods, and back to the truck. Only when she slows to a walk does she look over her shoulder, sizing me up.

"Good pace."

I choke on my own spit, coughing out something like a thanks. *Nice. Way to make a good impression, dipshit.*

Watters looks away before I can make any actual words come out, crossing to where Griggs waits, watching the rest slog up the hill. Some are striding out the last few paces, others are practi-cally falling over themselves with relief that it's over. I check my watch—we must have gone five miles. I watch anxiously until

Jason finishes, shaking out my arms and legs, stretching my hip flexors and IT bands. I've never been more tired in my entire life, but the jitters are good and gone. A slow smile stretches across my face. I made it through the first twenty-four hours. How much harder can it get?

Fifty years ago, California's fire seasons fit neatly into a range of blistering summer months. A long one, sure, with plenty of time for wildfire to lick across the land. But the summers were cooler and the lakes higher. The buildup in the understory was modest, still. Only a smattering of cabins dotted the wild spaces.

These days it's a steady march of structures from the cities into the hills. And it isn't like up north, where snow and heavy rains put an end to one season before the next begins. Now, fire season never ends, not really.

Every time, the question becomes: Defend the structure or attack the fire? Work to contain the blaze or fight to save a life?

CHAPTER 13

GRIGGS GIVES US fifteen minutes to shower when we get back to the base. I stumble out of the truck, fatigue from the long overnight shift and the morning run stealing the strength from my legs. Jason clamps onto my elbow. He's swaying, too, and maybe I'm holding him up as much as he's steadying me. I blink until, after a few dizzy moments, my head clears.

Tired as I am, the part of my brain that has been buzzing with excitement since I got to base kicks into gear. I hurry inside the dorm, grab a fresh set of Nomex, a clean pair of socks, underwear, and a dry bra, and hit the shower. It's one of those old-school ones where opaque tile walls divide a row of four shower stalls, each with industrial vinyl curtains across the narrow end. For once, being the only female in the crew works in my favor—I have a shower room all to myself, meaning there's nobody to see the hardware jabbed into my abdomen.

I throw my clothes down, hang up my towel, and turn

on the water while I peel off the filthy clothes I spent the last twenty-four hours in. With everybody trying to shower at the same time, I can't count on having anything close to hot water, or even lukewarm, for long. Even so, I sway in the steam, my head nodding and snapping as I fight off sleep standing up. I could have stayed in there for an hour at least, letting the stream pulverize my poor muscles, but no way am I going to be late on the second day of training. I shut off the water and rub myself down—gently, considering the fresh bruises that bloomed overnight.

I dress quickly, then rake a comb through my hair, squeeze out most of the water, and section it into a wet braid. I rummage in the back of my closet for the locked medical box, find my glucometer, prick my finger, and insert the test strip. I'm shaking with exhaustion while I wait for the readout. The pump and sensor haven't failed me yet, but after a twenty-four hour stint like the one we just endured, I can't be too sure. The glucometer beeps in a satisfying range and I can breathe easy. I stuff the kit back out of view, then rub a layer of sunscreen onto my face and neck, slap my cheeks, and hustle back outside.

Griggs waits for us in the shadow of the gaping ready-room door. When the last person shuffles in a few seconds before the old clock on the wall ticks straight up to mark the hour, he orders, "Suit up."

We help each other wrangle into our jumpsuits while he continues. "Prior to every jump, you'll perform two safety checks: one before you enter the aircraft, and one before you exit the aircraft. You will not *run* through these checks, not ever. Any risk you take up there puts your entire crew in danger, so you will treat each and every element of those checks as the single most important thing you will do that day."

He taps the clipboard with the butt of his pen. "This job is not for the careless. It is not for the negligent. The only way we avoid fatalities is if we treat every single procedure like it's life and death."

"I'm pretty sure having no sense of humor is life and death, too," Jason mutters.

"Shut up," I whisper.

Griggs scans the group and notices my lips moving. "What's that—Scott? Blair Scott. Is something I said funny?"

"No, sir." *Shit.* "Just repeating your words so I remember them: *every procedure is life and death.*"

Griggs nods, his lips tight.

I am going to kill Jason.

"And it is your job to do an informal visual check of the other jumpers on the plane with you at every opportunity. Now grab a checklist off the table, turn to a partner, and take turns assuming the role of spotter and jumper."

I swivel to glare at Jason, swiping a checklist for us to share and jamming it into his chest.

"Sorry."

"Seriously. Now?"

"I know. Dialing the sarcasm down to zero—at least when that clipboard is in view." Jason smirks, and we start in on the checklist.

Griggs wanders through the room while we practice. Then, once he's satisfied, it's on to pre-jump aircraft procedures. And since everybody is already suited up in our marshmallow suits, we go outside to practice our first parachute landing falls—PLFs. We start in a line spaced several feet apart in the grass while Griggs shouts instructions.

"Feet together, aaaand jump." We land with a rumble.

"Again. Keep those knees bent."

We jump again.

"This time, as your feet hit the ground, you're going to fall onto your hip, rolling as much as you can."

I sneak a glance at Jason. Sure enough, he's grinning. All those years of tackle practice—the guy could fall a dozen different ways without hurting himself.

"Feet together, jump, roll. That's better. Now watch. This time you're going to finish that roll by kicking your feet—still together—into the air so that your roll goes from your thigh around your hip and onto your back. Watch again." Griggs jumps, collapsing as he lands into a side roll, and ending on his back like a turtle.

"You go at your own pace; I'll come around to correct your positioning."

I put my head down and let my body work it out. My face goes red as a beet—the jumpsuits don't breathe for shit. After the night we had, my muscles are not thanking me for banging them onto the ground repeatedly. I clench my teeth as I hit the ground for the umpteenth time. Deep-tissue massage. Feels fan-freaking-tastic.

Griggs's voice sounds over my left shoulder. "The last thing you'll do before you touch down is work those steering lines so you're facing into the wind. If you don't, the roll will be twice as hard, and more than likely, your forward momentum plus the wind will throw you down flat on your face."

I make some adjustments and try again. Oof.

He walks through the group one more time, calling out corrections, and berating one of the young guys named Luís for not finishing his rolls on his back. But Griggs must be moderately satisfied because he calls a halt after maybe twenty minutes and directs us to a set of wooden blocks with ramps attached.

"Form two lines behind the blocks. Most jumps will be executed in two-person teams, called sticks. The spotter will signal the first person in the stick, then you'll both jump. We'll practice a few times so you can get used to the added height and velocity. A couple feet may not seem like much, but the additional momentum may help some of you finish those rolls. And even from this height, you only have to forget to bend your knees once to learn that lesson good. You may have braces on your ankles, but there's nothing to keep you from jamming your hip into the socket. I've only seen that happen once, and let me tell you, I'd never heard a human being scream like that."

I step up to the block, every muscle protesting. I listen for the count, then jump, and slam down on my already bruised hip. I roll and kick myself back to standing. Everything hurts, but I breathe into the pain. I can handle pain. What I can't handle is getting cut on my second day.

Give clear instructions
and be sure they are understood.

CHAPTER 14

THAT AFTERNOON, AFTER I inhale my lunch like something out of a cartoon, they put us through our first classroom session. I stuff the last bite of a brownie into my cheek; temperamental glucose levels be damned. I've earned some gooey deliciousness. I glance around the room, counting. Sixteen. Yep—one more guy is gone, with no explanation.

Jason leans across the aisle. "They're really cleaning house."

"Do you think it was the PLFs?"

He shrugs. "No idea."

At the front of the room, Hawkins scowls at the empty seats up front. "I see a couple candidates have already washed. Please, don't waste our time—if there's another one of you who'd rather mouth off than put your head down and learn what needs learning, there's the door."

He points, waiting, then clamps his hands on his hips when no one moves. "No? Well, don't get any ideas—classroom sessions are not nap time."

My watch vibrates: two pulses. Damn. Did I get my lunch carb intake wrong? Or am I just that depleted?

Hawkins is directly in front of me, near enough to hear my watch vibrate against the desk. I shift so I can cradle my wrist in my lap.

"Understanding fire from the ground and the air are two very different things. I expect you to listen, and be ready to apply what you learn today when you're out in the field."

When he gestures behind him and Watters steps forward, I stick my other hand into my chest pocket, grab two gummies, and slip them into my mouth. "You already know your trainer. What you may not know about her is that in the off-season, Watters teaches fire science classes at the university. So you'll want to pay close attention to what she has to say."

Watters passes around a stack of papers, then raps the extra handouts against the desk before beginning. "To understand where we are, you have to understand how we got here. In 1910, when the Big Blowup burned three million acres across the West, wildland fire became an enemy to be extinguished at all costs. So for the next half century or so, we fought fire, putting it out whenever possible.

"But the truth is that the land wants to burn; a healthy forest *needs* to burn. A moderate fire tends to clear fuel off the ground without destroying the canopy. If that fuel isn't periodically removed, it creates dangerous conditions—forests primed for the kind of megafires we're seeing today."

She moves around the room with the same coiled tension I saw yesterday in the moments before she took off at a run. But her face is no softer without those angular sunglasses hiding her gaze—if anything, the sharpness in her eyes makes the lines of brow, cheekbone, and jaw that much more intense.

I drop my gaze away from Watters's face as she pivots in my direction, then hurry to flip pages to catch up with the lecture. Heat flushes the sides of my neck, reaching for my cheeks and ears. *Quit. Embarrassing. Yourself.* For the rest of the session, I keep my eyes on that paper.

As I do, Watters talks about strategic mistakes from past years that resulted in loss of life, the advances in technology or fire science that have solved some problems, and the times when no one knows what went wrong. She stresses the constant need to justify the expense of smokejumpers to a public who maybe have never heard of them, and who definitely have no idea the number of forest fires they prevent each year.

"The unsettling truth is, fire is moving in new and unpredictable ways. In fifty years, classes just like this one will be learning about the mistakes we're making, now that we've got the twin problems of structural invasion into the forest and changing weather patterns."

Her gaze shifts to the window, eyes narrowing. "We don't know what's coming. And you can't prepare for what you don't understand. Scientists are modeling what they think wildland fire will be like if we don't curb climate change. But they're throwing darts at a target with blindfolds on. None of us can see into the future."

Fire Watch-Out Situations

No. 3: Safety zones and escape routes not identified.

CHAPTER 15

THE TOWERS I explored that first day on base loom overhead during every PT session. I've known the day was coming when the instructors would march us up there, so each morning while I sweat and grunt, pushing my body to its max, I prep mentally for what I know is coming. I just didn't plan for a heat wave.

It's one of those days when you can smell the heat, sharp and thick—like the grass beneath your feet just spontaneously combusted. Griggs's shirt is soaked in rings beneath his armpits and down the line of his back after leading us from the ready room to the first tower. Beneath my jumpsuit, I'm drenched by the time we leave the tarmac.

I stumble, mistiming a step on a perfectly flat surface. Anxiety spikes through me, slamming against my chest and prickling along my jawline. *Not now, please.*

My watch pulses. Shit. I can regulate my glucose levels without bringing too much attention to myself. But hydration—that's different. I can't stow extra canteens in every pocket. And if I get dehydrated, that messes with my readings and doses of insulin, meaning I can go into shock.

I'd never make it as a jumper in California's triple-digit temps—no way. We don't often get that kind of heat here. Just my luck it comes on a day when I'm depleted and stuffed into a Kevlar jumpsuit.

Griggs stops beneath the towers and points overhead. "This here is the landing simulator. Think about this session like boxing practice—if you never take any punches to the face, you won't be ready to step into the ring. Well, today you'll take your punches to the face."

Nobody even tries to hold back their groans.

"This is not the time to go joyriding. This is the time to remember what you learned about executing your PLFs; Watters will demonstrate."

My watch pulses again. Let me guess—my readings are bad because I'm dehydrated. Not a damn thing I can do about that now.

I watch through my metal face mask while Watters clips in and is hauled up the line. When the operator gives a signal, she begins to drop to the ground. Watters yanks on the stays to get herself turned just right, then plants her feet on the ground, rolling on impact.

I blink, trying to see through the flashes and dark spots in my vision.

"See," one of the guys behind me mutters, "that's why they call it the *slam*ulator. They reel you up like fish on a line and flop you on the ground, ready or not."

The guys chuckle. My pulse bangs against my skull, trying to get my attention. My watch vibrates again, insistent.

Griggs scowls. "Rather than joking around while you wait for your turn, I recommend you pay attention to the others. When you see somebody make a mistake, be sure you can identify what they did wrong and how you can get it right." Griggs jerks his thumb at Luís. "You're up. Remember, keep your feet together, and do not lock your knees."

After Luís, a stocky nineteen-year-old from SoCal, it's Xander's turn. He's a lanky guy one year older than me who's got a runner's lean build. Next up are three of the older guys: one they call Norris because of his ginger goatee and obsession with martial arts; after that comes Trout, who got that name due to something that happened in the guys' bathroom on the first night; and then the dude with a mangy ponytail named Russell— whether that's his first or last name, I'm not sure.

One by one the guys are hefted up the cables, then dropped, fast and hard, to the ground. Our suits are thick and padded, but some beatings can't be softened by any amount of padding. We're all going to be nursing bruises tonight and considering ourselves lucky if that's the worst of it.

When it's my turn, Jason claps me on the back. "You got this."

Do I? My mouth is dry as kindling. I soaked through my clothes inside that furnace of a suit and my head is still pounding away. Tuck and roll—that's all I have to do. Hang like a rag doll, then tuck and roll. And then I can make some excuse about having to pee, down a gallon or two of water, check my levels, and try again.

Somebody straps me in and clips me to the cable, shouting instructions. I can't slap my own cheeks through the face shield to wake myself up; instead I bite down on the inside of my cheek. With a jerk, I'm lifted off the ground and drawn into the air. My hands fly up to grip the parachute trails, not that it'll do a bit of good. I resist the urge to flail my legs—when you can't control your body, trying to change that fact only looks like panic.

And I don't have any room in my brain for panic—I can't think clearly enough for that. The pounding in my head finally quits—like it's given up on saving me from myself. But my watch is a constant flare, furious that I'm ignoring its warnings.

I'm all the way up at the top of the cables, peering over at the tower when, with another jerk, I start flying downhill. A faint breeze washes over my cheeks, clearing my mind enough so that as the ground rears up to meet me, I remember to smack my feet together. But when my boots hit the ground, instead of buckling and rolling along my side and onto my back, I slam face-first into the dirt.

My chest seizes—and for a moment, I can't make sense of anything. My eyes bug out, my mouth opening and closing to no effect. My pulse roars in my ears like a crackling fire, burning up any rational thought in my head, scorching my throat and sending beads of sweat running down my ribs and temples and the base of my neck.

After what feels like an eternity, the spasms begin to loosen and I draw in a loud, gasping breath. It scrapes against my parched throat and I roll onto my hands and knees, sucking in breath after blessed breath.

I haul myself upright, still breathing deep. Everyone is staring.

"You okay, Blair?" one of the guys asks—the one who's always goofing off whenever the trainers aren't looking. Yolo, I think?

"Yep," I gasp. "I just need to catch my breath. And water. Let me at it one more time, then I need some water."

Griggs smacks his clipboard against his thigh. "I shouldn't have to tell you, conditions out there will be a hundred times worse than here on base. If you can't remember to properly hydrate before a jump—"

"I can." I wave his hands away from the clips below my collarbone. "Ready."

"Blair, come on. Just take a break." Jason's face swims in and out of focus.

"I'm fine." And still clipped in. So with a yank, I'm lifted into the air again. I grip the stays, swaying. Too soon, they release me and I plummet toward the ground again.

No way—

I slap my feet together.

—*am I washing out*—

I yank the stays.

—*because I need a drink of goddamn water.*

I twist when my boots touch down, kicking high as I roll onto my back. When Griggs turns away with a satisfied grunt, my head drops, and I sag in relief. If I hurry, I can step away for a water break, then a quick manual reading while the rest of the guys finish. I heave myself upright and blink until everything stops spinning,

Rehydrate or you're done. I put one foot in front of the other and head back to the base.

That afternoon, when we're finally released for lunch, Jason sits me down on the bench while he runs to get food for us both. While he's gone, Trout and Russell walk by with two guys whose names I haven't bothered to learn yet.

"Females." Trout shakes his head.

"Weak," Russell mutters.

It's not the first time I've heard that shit. Still, it burns, every time. But I won't waste one scrap of energy lashing out. I need all of it to back myself away from this cliff. And I can use the rage later, when my body is my own again. For now, I stare at the knot of wood on the table in front of me because I'm too damn tired to do anything else. I trace the spiral, coiling inward, with my finger.

The guys scatter when Jason returns with two waters, a carton of chocolate milk, and some pink electrolyte drink.

"You're going to down all four of those while I watch."

"Okay, jeez."

He tears into his sandwich, eyebrows raised, while I take down the first water. I bite into my sandwich next but can't taste a thing. The last thing I feel like doing is eating. Or drinking.

"What the hell, Blair?" he mutters around his bites. "You could have taken a freaking water break. They weren't going to wash you because you were dehydrated."

"You don't know that." My voice sounds chalky. I can't seem to form words—my tongue is in the way.

"You shouldn't have gone back up there. You should have listened to me *for once*, gone to the back of the line, chugged a few canteens of water, and then tried again once you could see straight."

"Maybe. Maybe not."

"Just—don't talk. Drink."

Jason is such a nag when he's worried. "Thanks."

I get a glare for that. "You can thank me when you don't pass out this afternoon."

He's right—and being stubborn won't help me one bit. I pick the chocolate milk next. The carbs will help, and my muscles will thank me for that later.

"Yeah, so I won't pass out, but I'll get cut for having to pee twelve times during the classroom session."

Jason smiles around his next bite. He waves at someone across the way, then slaps the table beside us. He's always been quick to make friends. Me—not so much.

"Blair, these two are in my section of the dorm." I look up as they settle onto the bench—two of the older candidates, probably in their late twenties, both lean and chiseled, like they spend every spare second in the weight room.

The one across from me dips his head. "I'm Ysidro, but everybody calls me Yolo."

Right.

"Dirk" is all the guy next to me says.

"Hey." I already know I like Dirk. He keeps quiet and doesn't give me any shit for being a girl. And Yolo—well, everybody likes him.

"That's enough chatter from you." Jason jams the second water into my palm.

"Yeah, yeah." But I tip it back and drink, slowly, so all that liquid doesn't come right back up again.

Yolo looks between the two of us. "This your girlfriend, or what?"

Jason covers his nose to keep from shooting chocolate milk all over the place. While he coughs and bangs on his chest, I answer.

"Nope. We grew up together, two houses down."

Dirk nods, but still doesn't add so much as a grunt to the conversation.

"So like brother and sister, then."

"Sort of, yeah."

"Best friends." Jason grins. "Matching lockets and all."

Yolo laughs, slapping the table. My face feels like it's on fire. I never understood how Jason can do that—wear his emotions on his sleeve like it's the most natural thing in the world.

"Seriously, Blair's the best." Jason coughs, banging on his chest one last time. "Forget about this morning—she may be thirty pounds lighter than any of the three of us, but she's going to kick all our asses in at least half the units. Just watch."

Yolo turns a thoughtful eye toward me. "So what happened earlier?"

"I got dehydrated. Couldn't think straight. I guess when we

got going again after the all-nighter, I should have focused on downing some water."

"And you're paying for it now." Scoldy Jason is back.

I finish off my sandwich and reach for the electrolytes. "I'm feeling better already, thanks to Nurse Jason here. Believe me, that will not be a mistake I make again. Ever." I stand, lunging over the bench. Time to log all those carbs so my insulin pump can get to work evening out my blood sugar before my watch pulses a hole straight through my wrist.

"Now, if you don't mind, I've got to pee."

Smokejumper Parachute Types

main: The primary parachute used by smokejumpers; positioned on the individual's back to be deployed upon exit from the aircraft.

reserve: The secondary parachute to be used in emergency situations; positioned on the jumper's chest and deployed manually by pulling a red handle.

round (FS-14): The traditional parachute used by smokejumpers since the program's inception.

square (Ram-Air): The predominant parachute structure used by today's smokejumpers; allows for deployment in higher wind conditions.

CHAPTER 16

BRIGHT AND EARLY the next morning, Watters takes us out on a six-mile run. My brain is slow to wake, but my body relishes the steady beat of my blood flowing, my breath pumping, and my feet striking the ground. I become a different person in those moments—softer, more fluid, the fight I'm always bracing for forgotten.

After the other runners fall back a few paces, I catch up to Watters and our strides fall into an easy rhythm. Maybe I only imagine the static sparking between us. Maybe she doesn't set her pace to the cadence of my footfalls.

Of course she doesn't. Quit being ridiculous.

All I know is, when the run ends and she peels away without a word, I feel that snap of separation like a physical thing.

PT doesn't end with the run. Watters takes us to the obstacle course next, demonstrating each section and finishing by pulling a fire shelter over her body.

"Under three minutes every time, that's your goal."

I eye the course, moving through each part in my head. Junior year, I talked the track coach into adding a decathlon to the events our high school team competed in, even though I was it—the only girl on the team who signed up. This doesn't seem so different.

Watters lines us up and sends us out, then crosses to the army-crawl station to pick up a couple of sticks so she can bang them against the bars over our heads to rattle us while we struggle underneath. At the far end, Griggs simulates a gusting burnover by trying to shake the fire shelter out of each candidate's hands. I pace myself the first time through to get a feel for each trial, how best to approach and execute each one.

Jason catches me grinning after the first lap and rolls his eyes. "You're nuts, you know that?"

I burst out laughing. "Yeah."

"Something funny?" Griggs appears over my shoulder. "Obviously we aren't working you hard enough. Okay, rooks, anyone coming in over the three-minute mark gets to run it two more times."

Fine by me. I get going again, pushing myself this time to take the course at my top speed. But when I drop to the ground for the army crawl, a hand shoves my head into the sandpit. I jerk my face free, spitting and panting to slough off the sudden panic.

"Why don't you keep your mouth shut," Trout mutters.

He moves past me. Once I can breathe again, I crawl steadily to the far end, stuffing down boiling rage. I shoot to my feet, then speed up my knee-highs through the tires and lunge up and over the wall. Cursing under my breath, I sprint through the last set of obstacles. I finish by pulling my fire shelter over my body and hanging on while they try to yank it out of my hands. When I hop up and check my time, I'm still seething. I glance around for Trout. Who does he think—

But everybody has stopped whatever they were doing on the O-course, their attention fixed on the backside of the wall where one of the candidates is rolling on the ground hissing, his ankle cupped between his hands. His face twists in pain as he tries not to cry out.

"Zeb, Kurt, help him back to the office." Watters sweeps her gaze over the fifteen of us left. "Freak accidents can happen to anybody, to the most fit person out here, at any time. It isn't enough in this job to be the fastest or strongest or toughest, not if you don't take care to be smart, too. If you can't be meticulous in everything you do, whether it's your pack, your chute, or your own body you're seeing to, this job isn't for you."

All around me, the guys shift uneasily, still breathing hard.

"Run it again," she says, picking up her sticks and banging them against the bars. "And this time be quick *and* careful."

We take off again, just as hard, and just as fast. But this time, the jeers and the heckling stop. The only sound is tight, controlled breathing, and somehow, softer landings. Focus—that's what it sounds like.

When at last Watters is satisfied, she calls us into a huddle.

"Look, I know it feels like we're here to make your life a misery—that we want you to fail. But the truth is, it's the opposite. This is a hell season we're in the middle of; there's no other way to say it. Any other year if you get hurt in camp—sure, you might wash out, but you'll go home, heal up, and be back to fighting fires later in the season. But the region simply can't afford to send more folks home this year on account of preventable injuries. You have to be honest with us and with yourselves. If your body isn't up to this, we need you back on your rappeller or hotshot crew. We need every able body fighting these fires."

It's some kind of sick joke that after lunch, when human beings want nothing more than to curl up in a little sunshine and doze off, is also a fire's hottest hour, when it'll travel the farthest distance in the shortest amount of time. It's also when my blood sugar tends to dip.

When we show up in the loft after lunch, the guy with the sprained ankle is gone. Griggs has a chute stretched out on the long, narrow table in front of him. He shows us how round, square, and reserve chutes are packed.

I can barely keep my eyes open. I bite down on my cheek to keep from yawning. That doesn't work. I pinch the inside of my arm with my fingernails to try to force myself alert—are my levels that low? I thought I was being so careful. That's what makes living with diabetes so tricky—you can be doing everything right but your own body is fighting you, all the time.

Griggs shows us how to check the canopy for structural problems, how to be sure the lines won't tangle on exit, and finally, how to secure the bundle so it's ready to fly. At some point a sharp kick to my shin jolts me awake— "Ow!" Did I fall asleep? Standing up? Griggs glances around the room, trying to see what caused the sudden shout before going back to his monotone instructions. Only an idiot wouldn't pay attention to the part where you learn how not to drop out of the sky with a mangled chute. I tilt my head to the side, toward the direction of the well-timed kick.

"Thanks," I whisper.

"Don't mention it," Jason mutters.

Someday I am going to have to make it up to him for constantly saving my ass. The only problem is, my debts keep piling up, with no sign that things will ever balance out.

Montana on a road map is unremarkable, to say the least. There's the interstate cutting east to west and another north to south. A few cities of modest size. The long, firm line of the Canadian border.

But get your hands on a topographical map and Montana's wonders are plain to see. Sweeping valleys, rippling mountain ranges, cool rivers cutting through the land. Try to look at that map—see if you can peer into the expanses of untamed land without your fingers trailing along the curving lines, without leaning in to peer closer, without the hunger building inside you to lose yourself in all that wilderness.

CHAPTER 17

EARLY THE NEXT morning, the trainers drive us north of the base so Watters can take us up a brutal hill run. Then, once we're good and tired, Griggs hikes us deep into the forest and throws his gear down at the base of a big-ass tree.

"When you exit the aircraft, you aim for a preselected clearing, and if all goes as it should, you land in some long grass with a couple rocks sprinkled in, just to make things interesting. If things go badly, you might end up dangling from a tree. And believe me when I tell you, falling out of that tree is much more dangerous than jumping out of an airplane. For one thing, there's no chute to slow you down. For another, the branches below you are just as likely to knock you out as slow your fall. And while you might land on a pillow of pine needles, you could also impale yourself on a broken tree limb."

He fastens a climbing harness around his waist and thighs, straps a pair of spurs to his boots, and after a rigorous safety check, begins climbing. "Point being, you do not want to fall out of that tree."

He clips into a rope looped around the back of the trunk, flips it up higher than his waist, steps the spurs into the wood, and begins climbing. Flip, step, step, and repeat. He looks like a woodcutter in one of those grainy Depression-era photos posing a hundred feet in the air, trusting nothing more than a pair of heel spurs to keep him up there.

Griggs talks while he climbs, using quick, sure movements, and calling instructions over his shoulder. "Once you're hung up, you need to know how to tie yourself off and lower yourself to the ground—we'll do letdowns in a few days. Today's all about how to get back up there and reclaim your chute."

Nobody in their right mind would sign up for smoke-jumper training if they were afraid of heights, but this isn't some easy-to-climb oak tree with low-hanging branches. This is a two-hundred-foot-tall pine tree.

"I'd take jumping out of planes any day," Jason mutters.

Griggs is so high up, he has to shout to be heard. "It's no different from anything else we've taught you. You do it right the first time. There's no other option. Try to go too fast and you'll make a mistake."

He ties a bandana near the top before making his way carefully downward. When he drops to the ground at last, Griggs nods. "Who's up?"

Shit. Here we go. I take a step forward.

"Are you nuts?" Jason hisses.

I flash him a smile, hoping it doesn't look too much like a grimace. "Probably."

Climbing half prepared isn't the worst thing I can imagine. Waiting on the ground, my nerves shouting at me while the guys take their turn—most doing way better than me because they know their way around climbing gear—that would be a million times worse. Or my blood sugar spiking one way or another and betraying me again. Besides, I really need to impress Griggs after almost nodding off yesterday during the classroom session.

I turn my back on the others to hide my shaking hands while I cinch the harness around my thighs and lash it across my waist. I don't know where my courage went or why, exactly, it chose this moment to abandon me, but I'll fake it if I have to. I clip into the flip line while Griggs checks the shin straps on my spurs. Then he steps back, looking my equipment over one last time. "Well, what are you waiting for?"

I step up to the tree, feeling like I should offer the massive ponderosa some compliment or blood sacrifice or something so it won't be tempted to shake me loose. I close my eyes, leaning in for a whiff of that heady butterscotch smell. There, see? We aren't so unfamiliar with each other. Before I can think about it anymore, I sink the first spur into the wood and test my weight. Seems solid enough.

"Keep those knees bent around the trunk."

I sink the other spur into the wood, and just like that, I'm off the ground. I lock my right knee, move my hips snug against the bark and flip the line up above my waist, then lean back into the rope, notching my feet higher. Flip, notch, notch. I could get used to this—if I can keep my brain from freaking out, and if I can remember to focus on the tree instead of the steadily increasing distance from the ground below.

"Watch it," Griggs calls up. "Sink your spur into a crack like the one by your right knee and it'll never hold. Take your time to find a solid placement."

I hiss a breath through my teeth—I didn't even see that crack. *Focus, Blair.*

Stores of sap from deep within the tree leach through creases in the bark, their scent wafting into the dry air, rolling over me in fragrant waves and tamping down the panic oozing from my pores. Maybe the tree recognizes the fire in me and, as is its nature, soothes the burn before it can overtake either of us.

Every so often, I have to unclip the folded pruning saw from my harness and trim away a limb or stub jutting out from the bark.

"Keep any pruning action nice and high—well away from the rope that's keeping you from falling to the ground."

I grimace, adjusting my aim with the saw. Does that guy ever consider offering suggestions without attaching a threat of imminent death?

When I reach the crown, fingers extended and trembling, to touch the bandana Griggs tied there, I close my eyes for a moment, swaying a little. Done. Now I just have to get myself back onto solid ground. Going down is much easier than up—I've already cleared the limbs, and I know what spots on the tree to avoid. The hardest part is convincing myself to take it slow.

When my feet finally hit the ground and I unclip, I have to reach out and steady myself against the trunk while a flood of relief knocks my knees together, draining the blood from my head. I blink away spots in my vision while a couple guys clap me on the shoulder. Jason only glares, cupping a hand under my elbow to make sure I stay upright.

After Griggs scribbles something on his clipboard, he makes a big show of checking his watch. "Twenty minutes." He looks at the others waiting their turn. "So if anyone needed help understanding why the last thing you want is to land in a tree—*if* you survive the letdown and you're healthy enough to climb back up and retrieve your gear—you have just lost precious time that could have been spent setting up camp, hiking in to the fire, or even beginning your initial attack."

Trout sidles around my other side. In a voice pitched low enough so no one else can hear, he mutters, "Hear that? You only slow us down. Do us all a favor and quit playing with fire, why don't you."

I keep my gaze forward, fixed on Griggs. I'd like nothing more than to shut Trout's smug mouth with my fists—but that would play right into his hand. I breathe through flared nostrils, clenching and unclenching my hands instead.

Griggs looks west, toward the thick of the wilderness. "Out there, twenty minutes is the difference between life and death. Twenty minutes is the difference between a lightning strike that's snuffed before it can really get going, and a wildfire that destroys a hundred thousand acres. Remember, it isn't only you who you're hurting if you get injured out in the wilderness, it's your whole crew. All of a sudden, you're not on a mission to stop a fire from getting out of control. Your entire crew is now on a rescue mission to get the injured party out safely." Another pause—Griggs loves a dramatic pause. "So don't be the asshole who chutes directly into a tree, okay?"

Fire Watch-Out Situations

No. 1: Fire not scouted and sized up.

CHAPTER 18

BY THE END of the tree-climbing session, we all need to blow off some steam. Everybody made it up that damn tree and back down again, and that's worth celebrating. Some of the guys were up and down fast, without breaking a sweat, and some were slower like me, and shaking a little, too. Maybe it's mean, but seeing them struggle makes me feel a little better. After showering away the panic sweat, we drive into town for a steak dinner where all of us rookies eat together at one long table—like friends, almost.

After dinner, the group splits up. The older guys head for the bar, while the four of us still underage park it outside the A&W next door. Jason and I sit on the curb, watching the occasional pickup truck roll by. I lean back to give my overfull belly room to stretch out, eyeing my leftovers with regret—there's just no room left for those chili fries.

Luís hops off the picnic table, taking a few steps toward the bar. "Let's go in there. The rest of the rookies will never take us seriously if we act like kids."

I look away. I'll already feel that steak on my morning run—and I splurged on those mashed potatoes. No way am I adding alcohol to my already stressed systems.

"No, thanks." Jason stabs his straw into the bottom of his empty cup.

"Aw, come on, goody-goodies, it's only a beer."

I glance sidelong at Jason. His eyebrows jump—he obviously wants to say yes.

"Go on—I'll wait here."

He stands, dusting off his butt. Before he joins the others, he kicks the sole of my runners. "You sure?"

"Oh my god," Egan mutters.

"I'm good." I fold my arms over my knees and rest my chin in the crook of one elbow. Then I'm alone on the curb, which is fine by me.

"Idiots," I mutter once they're out of earshot. A complicated medical condition isn't the only reason not to drink during training. No way are Watters and Griggs going to let up in the morning. And with how exhausted everybody is, even a little alcohol will sap their muscles of energy.

The traffic slows, not that there was much to begin with. The sky dims, and the bugs start piping up. I get so caught up following one thought trail where it forks into another and circles back around that I don't even hear footsteps approaching until the toe of a familiar pair of runners nudges the side of my knee.

I look up, squinting a little at the streetlight as Watters's face blots out the glare.

"Oh. Um, hi."

She nods, looking from me to the empty picnic table and the even emptier parking lot. "You get stranded out here in the big city?"

I duck my head, hiding a smirk. Who knew Watters had anything resembling a sense of humor?

"No."

She looks toward the bar and back down at me again, switching her bag of groceries to the other hip. "I'd offer you a ride back to base . . ."

I'm working up to saying no, mostly because I don't know what the hell we'd talk about for a whole twenty minutes alone, but Watters shoots down the idea before I have the chance to open my mouth.

". . . but you've got a good chance at making it through training. And if I help you, even a little, even off base, people will assume you didn't earn that spot. It shouldn't be that way, but it is."

I stand up slowly, dusting gravel off my jeans. Without the

streetlight throwing Watters's face into shadow, I can see the darts between her eyebrows and the hard line of her jaw—so serious, all the time.

"You think I've got a good shot?"

Her lips thin in disapproval. "I didn't mean . . . Look, everybody has a shot. All that age crap aside, you wouldn't be here if somebody out there didn't believe you could hack it."

She really thinks that? I duck my eyes away, and raise up on my tiptoes to peer into her grocery bag. Jerky, protein powder, bananas, and . . . "Cookies? Pretty sure the trainer on base wouldn't approve."

That almost gets a smile. "I'll have you know, Fig Newtons are better for endurance than most of those fancy energy bars you all waste your money on. Lighter weight, too. Those days on the fire line when you're tempted to take a bite out of a tree to get some more calories in you, a half dozen of these will keep you going."

"No kidding?"

She shakes her head. "I'd offer you some, but—"

"Yeah, yeah. Favoritism. Sexism. Whatever-other-ism."

Watters chuckles, finally backing away. "I'm serious."

"I know." Pretty sure I'm grinning like an idiot.

Pressure builds under my ribs. Warm. Inviting.

Stop that.

Watters turns away without another word and makes for her dusty blue pickup. It has rust spots on the wheel wells, a rifle in the cab window, and a padlocked gear box weighing down the back. She probably has her pack and boots stowed in there, too—most seasoned firefighters keep the basics at hand wherever they go so they're never caught unprepared.

I stand under the streetlight, trying to yank my gaze away, as Watters slides into the truck, shuts the door, starts the engine, and rolls away without looking back once.

Not her.

Shut it down, Blair.

I stare after the truck, wishing I'd thought to ask why Watters chose training incoming rookies instead of jumping fires, when I realize I'm not alone on the sidewalk anymore.

"You ratted us out, didn't you?" Luís looks pissed.

Egan groans. "I knew she was going to bring us down eventually."

"Shut up, both of you," Jason practically growls.

I roll my eyes. "Watters went to the grocery store. We talked about Fig Newtons—sorry if it hurts your ego that we didn't spend that three-second conversation talking about you."

Then I turn on my heel and make for the truck before anyone can say another word. I'm not going to get dragged into any of that bullshit.

But I can feel Jason watching me walk away. He and I don't lie to each other, and since I'm not ready to fess up to anything I'm thinking or trying like hell to stop feeling, it's better not to give him the chance to say anything.

A big fire makes its own weather. With temperatures cresting at three thousand degrees, steamy air rises into the atmosphere, where it cools, condensing into fire clouds: great hulking gray pyrocumulus reaching miles above the blaze. Updrafts of smoke rivaling the plumes from volcanic eruptions form even greater clouds that spit lightning and still-burning embers below, spreading the flames even farther.

And the fire makes its own wind. On its borders, the wind may be clocked at a modest fifteen miles per hour, while inside the fire, whipped into a frenzy by the heat and the flames themselves, gusts and twisters can reach 140 miles per hour.

Nothing spreads a fire faster than wind.

CHAPTER 19

I'M NOT SHY about kicking everyone's ass in map-and-compass training the following day—even Egan the Eagle Scout, which really pisses him off. Aunt Cate trained me well, and I've always been good at tactile stuff like that. I like being able to hold the thing in my hand, see it move when I move, and watch the lines on the map come to life in the terrain all around me. I'm good at it—really good.

The afternoon classroom session is all about steering parachutes—when to reach for the toggles, what to do in gusty situations, and the transition from round chutes to squares. Like every afternoon, I have to fight falling asleep for the whole first hour of class while my watch pulses at me until I reach just the right glucose level.

Once we're finally released for the evening, Jason and I head for an empty corner of the parking lot. The base is a far cry from a fire camp—no grassy field to stretch out in, no tent camp full of other teenagers. It's as cozy as an airport, what with commercial planes taking off overhead at regular intervals. Still, it's our thing.

I settle into my camping chair, ready for some music, but what I get instead is a lecture. Another tradition, apparently.

"Come on, you gotta cool it with that macho stuff, always jumping to the front of the line. I always learn something from the hotheads"—he shoots me a pointed look—"who go first."

I roll my eyes, making a show of buffing the harmonica, though it's already clean as a whistle.

"Seriously. Watching a few people go before me—and taking note of when and how they mess up—it makes me better when my turn comes around. You should give it a try."

He doesn't get it. "Come on. People look at that big hulk of a body you've got and they know you belong here, despite your age. They assume the opposite of me. I *have* to prove myself. Every single day. Every chance I get."

Jason shakes his head. He starts strumming a familiar chord progression, his mouth twisting up at the corners.

Dammit. "Don't you dare—"

He cuts me off, singing around a cheesy grin. " 'Slow down, you crazy child . . . ' "

It's that Billy Joel song about the hothead who doesn't know when to stop.

"I'm walking away." I pocket the harmonica and drag my

camping chair behind me, stomping away like a three-year-old.

"Wait," he calls. "*Blair*. Come back!"

"You're an asshole," I call over my shoulder.

"Yes." He doesn't quit laughing, though.

I stop and turn halfway back. "And a nag."

"The naggiest."

With a huff, I drag my chair back beside his and plunk onto it. "No more Billy Joel."

"I can't make that promise."

"Fine—no more using Billy Joel to take jabs at me."

"Deal." He ducks his head and mutters, "For tonight."

I punch his bicep, hard enough that he won't be strumming anything for at least fifteen minutes.

He howls, still chuckling. "Gimme your notebook. If your glucose levels are all over the place, it isn't only you who Aunt Cate is going to murder."

I hand it over and put my feet up—let him look over the numbers and do all the worrying. Serves him right.

Maintain prompt communications with your forces, your supervisor, and adjoining forces.

Standard Firefighting Orders, No. 7

CHAPTER 20

ALL THOSE FOREST Service roads outside of town go on forever into the wilderness. Probably clear on to Canada, if you've got the legs to make it there. It must be why the trainers like to run us along that endless web of trails; there's no way of knowing whether Watters will call a halt after two miles or ten. We never know if we're headed out on a loop, or out and back, or on a straight run where a truck will pick us up right when we're about to collapse.

It's a control thing. If you know how much pain is coming, you can plan for it; you can ration your energy, or at least you can trick your mind into thinking you can. But that's the thing about rookie training—they're not only preparing us for the physical challenges and tactical understanding we'll need. They're forcibly molding us into the kind of person who can take all manner of mental beatings, too.

So they'll say we've got a classroom session in the afternoon, only to direct us to the O-course again. Or they'll pull us out of PT just when we think it's finally over and send us on a six-mile pack hike up a mountain.

The unpredictability is killer.

While Griggs calls roll, I lace up and stretch at the back of the group. Watters prances in place, light on her toes, like she can't wait to get going. Though I told myself I wouldn't look, my gaze sticks there—she's so strong. It's . . . impressive. Beautiful—

"Blair?"

My head snaps up. "Here." Everyone's staring. Shit.

"You sure about that?"

"Yes, sir."

Griggs taps his pen against the clipboard, scowling. Super-fit people can look angry by default—maybe it's only the lack of body fat in the cheeks that makes him always seem so . . . severe.

"Drop your packs, hardhats, gloves, and boots in the trucks. You'll need them later."

Watters springs forward, at a faster pace than she's ever set. Like every training run, the guys thunder after her, their footfalls heavy. Half of them either have never learned how to pace themselves, or don't care, which is fine by me—let them tire themselves out at the start.

Within a half mile, we're surrounded by trees. The forest calms me, makes my breath deeper, softens my jaw, and lightens my step. I glance around from my spot at the back of the pack—I'm not concerned about my pace, only with keeping distance between myself and Yolo's flailing limbs. That guy needs a lesson in form—badly.

It's a healthy forest. Not too congested with blowdowns or crawling underbrush—which figures. This close to base, it's probably been combed over regularly by trainees. The sun is still low enough that it dips in and out of sight off to my left, sending streamers of light slipping through the trees. If there's any wildlife nearby, it scatters at the sound of our footfalls on the crushed gravel.

Sure enough, after the second mile, the pack begins to stretch out, the slowest falling behind. It isn't about lungs—anybody who can work a fire line through the middle of the night at the pace we did on our first day here should be able to handle distance runs. But some of them are too muscle-bound to be efficient, while others have horrible form and even worse breath control.

I jog out to the side and pass three of them, settling in beside Jason. He can handle runs; he just doesn't like them. I stay with him for a minute or so before surging past the next few stragglers. Jason and I are not good running partners. He can wipe the floor with me when it comes to sprints but doesn't have a chance at keeping up with me over any distance. His stride is a good foot longer than mine, for one. And a cloud of grump surrounds him whenever he has to run more than a mile or two. Another time, I'd poke that bear, see if I can get a rise out of him. But if I want him to make it through training—and of course I do—the best thing I can do is leave him alone with his misery and focus on myself. No way am I giving Griggs any more reasons to call me out.

So I stretch out to join the lead pack. Watters's stub of a ponytail bobs at the front. She isn't in training, so she can wear whatever she wants. Today it's a silkweight crew neck top over running tights. I'm just happy we get to do this run in a T-shirt and shorts instead of Nomex.

With each stride, the back of the pack falls farther behind. I'll drag Jason up the hill if it comes to it, but all that "team" nonsense aside, I can't worry about the rest of them. I check my watch as we snake around a switchback and head uphill—we've gone five miles already. My mind settles, my breath flowing free, quieting any chatter or worry or spare thought. Screw meditation; wild spaces and working my body—that's the only way I've ever found something like peace.

The higher we climb, the more the sun makes itself known in openings in the canopy and bends in the road. When the road drops down again, we sink into shadows, and a moment of blessed cool. The guys at the back of the pack tend to scuff and slide in long strides on the downhill to make up lost ground. Those of us at the front do the opposite—tiny, quick steps to lessen the impact on our knees and to make it easier to regain our balance if a footfall skids out.

When the road flattens out, I check my watch again. Eight miles, at least. I feel better than I have in days, and without really meaning to, I begin to stride it out along the straightaway, forgetting why I'm there and who I'm with. It's just me, the road, and a pale swath of sky overhead. At some point I feel Watters beside me, like when you walk into what you think is an empty room, but you can sense that it isn't; you *feel* someone there.

It seems natural to hold there, matching Watters stride for stride. I let myself feel it, just for a moment, before drifting back a half step, settling for a place over her left shoulder. When the trucks come into view off a spur, Watters slows to a jog, then a walk, turning off the road and going to meet Griggs. I slow down, too, drifting away, recoiling as the distance between the two of us grows, any connection I thought I felt severed like a wayward thread.

I dig in my pack and fish out my canteen while Griggs and Watters mutter over the clipboard. They stand in the middle of the road, watching the rest of the recruits coming in. I duck my head, stretching some undetermined body part to hide my confusion. Watters didn't even look at me. Not a nod, or a *Good job*, or a *Nice run*. Nothing.

One by one, the others stumble toward the trucks. Before the last four guys even make it back, the rest of us suit up while Griggs walks us through the chainsaws jumpers use—how they're loaded into gear boxes and dropped out of the plane after the last stick, how jumpers have to know how to repair them in the field, then be able to pack them out with the rest of the gear. After that comes the crosscut saw, and we take turns learning to work the things in pairs. I've almost forgotten about the run by the time we get back to camp for lunch.

And then I realize—two of the guys who couldn't keep up are gone.

Most handcrews operate according to an established pecking order. The saw guys run the saws, every time. The rookies swing Pulaskis, every time. And there's a tool order to the line that never deviates. The person in command is the one with the most experience, nearly every time.

But not smokejumpers. The idea is, if you're badass enough to get accepted into training, and if you've got what it takes to survive that training, you must know what you're doing. You may be called a rookie for the first few years, but you've earned your place, same as everyone else.

That makes for a self-assured lot—you jump out of the plane, take care of your shit on landing, then go attack the fire as a team. Everybody is capable and everybody is at the top of their game, no pecking order necessary. Whoever is the first jumper out of the plane is the JIC—the jumper in charge—it's as simple as that.

CHAPTER 21

THE DAY TO practice letdowns comes during the second week of training, when I'm finally getting used to the weight of my jumpsuit. There are only thirteen of us left, meaning we'll each get more reps on the units. And that's a good thing—I can do PT until I'm blue in the face, but I need practice with all that technical stuff. My nerves spike, adrenaline rattling through me. All the guys who've rappelled out of helicopters for years are going to make this look like a walk in the park.

I need lots of reps—as many as I can get.

Griggs walks us to the tower and up the stairs. "As I've said before, jumpers try like hell not to get hung up in a tree, but it happens. Sometimes the jump spot is so small that if the wind shifts even a little, you'll miss it." He pats his right-leg pocket. "Your letdown rope should always be stowed in the same location."

Griggs clips himself in and swings out over empty air, demonstrating the process of securing the letdown rope, then unclipping from the chute and lowering himself to the ground. Then he calls for volunteers, and before I can heat up any more inside that Kevlar, I jump to the front of the line. Okay, so Jason's right about learning by watching. But I learn by doing. Besides, I can't let my nerves get the better of me.

I clip in and test my weight, then the pulley system floats me off the platform and over empty space. While Griggs calls out each step, I grit my teeth, shutting out everything but his voice, and keeping my eyes on my hands. My body moves through the motions and I count the passing seconds as I breathe in, then out, and do it again until the calm forced into my breath spreads through the rest of me.

I'm so focused on my hands and Griggs's shouted instructions, I don't even notice when I reach the ground. When my feet hit the layer of mulch, I jump, startled, and let out a low, shaky whistle. Now I only have to do that a million more times.

I unclip without looking up at the others waiting in the tower for their turn. They can't see my legs shaking from that distance, but I'm not going to risk letting anyone catch a glimpse of my face as that adrenaline fizzles out of me.

That night, Jason begs off our nightly ritual of decompressing under the stars and strumming pop music on a ukulele. He and Janie are veering sharply toward on-again, and they have a phone date lined up after dinner. I could wedge myself into whatever the other guys are up to, but as much as I'm coming to like a few of them, I need a break from all that testosterone.

So after double-checking my blood sugar logs and carefully tucking my notebook out of sight, I grab my puffy coat and head to the cafeteria, make a thermos of hot chocolate, and wander outside alone. The days are still scorching, but nights are beginning to dip into the forties. The crisp air taps my cheeks, nosing into the open space beneath my collar. The mountains in the distance swallow the lights of town—hunkering low and dark on the horizon. There is too much smoke in the air for the stars to make an appearance; the night sky glowers a dusty charcoal.

I do a loop, strolling around the outbuildings, the obstacle course, and the units. I finish outside Operations—candidates don't hang around in there during the day, but it's not like we aren't *allowed* inside, so long as nobody touches the jump list.

I jerk the front door open. A few lights are on, illuminating the hallways, but nobody seems to be around. I scuff across the carpet toward the opposite wall, where a whiteboard covers the wall behind a nondescript desk, with a series of color-coded magnets on the far left listing the active jumpers. To the right, the board notes the jumpers already dispatched to a fire or otherwise committed—so many called out of state on one big fire or another. My gaze swings back to the active jumpers.

I should get out of here—head back outside. But I can't help myself. I lean in.

There are slots for something like eighty people, but only twenty names are there to fill the open slots. It isn't uncommon for ten jumpers to load up for a single fire—no wonder they need our second class of rookies. Better to bench two trainers for six weeks if it gets you another dozen people ready to step in right when the fire season really heats up.

"Couple more weeks and maybe your name will be up there."

I jump, sloshing my hot chocolate across the desk. *"Shit."*

Watters launches out of a desk chair in the corner, chuckling. She grabs a roll of paper towels and helps me mop up the mess before it spills onto any of the carefully stacked paperwork. "I didn't mean to startle you."

"Says the lady lurking in the shadows."

Watters snorts with laughter.

I wipe down my hands and a few drips that splattered across my clothes. "Seriously, what are you doing sitting all alone in the dark?"

She blows out a long sigh. With a last swipe, she comes around the side of the desk, balling up the paper towels and chucking them over my shoulder into the trash. "Same as you, I'm guessing. Staring at my name on the wrong side of that whiteboard and wishing it was at the top of the jump list instead."

"You didn't want to be an instructor?"

She shrugs. "We're a team. Every one of us goes where we're asked to; we help in whatever way serves the crew best. I've got degrees in physio and fire science, so they could cut corners on classroom instructors with me pulling double duty. It's the same with Griggs—he's a master rigger and an EMT. But both of us would rather be out there."

Watters twists to look back at the list; suddenly we're standing hip to hip, whisper-close. Her eyes are fixed on the board—I suck in a breath and hold it, hoping the dim lighting hides that flush I feel creeping up the sides of my neck. I try to wrench my gaze away from the downy hairs, pale and practically invisible against the tanned skin beside her ear, and the cords of muscle along her neck, the bare triangle of skin at her collarbone. I should back away—even one step would dull the static. She feels it, too, doesn't she? How could she not?

Instead, I take a half step closer. Watters blinks, finally looking away from the board. Our noses are inches apart. Up close, her eyes aren't blue after all—they're gray, like glacial runoff: silty, glinting, opaque.

"Don't." Her voice is low, and cold. She steps away. "Clearly I was wrong—you don't care about your career. But no way in hell are you tanking mine with that shit."

I gasp, coming up for air. "I—"

But it's too late. The front door swings shut. She's gone.

Wildland Fire Categories

crown fire: Intense and destructive fires in which flames reach
the top of the trees; these fires spread rapidly through
the canopy in addition to, and at times in a different
direction from, any spread at the ground level.

ground fire: Slow-moving fires that burn fuel underground;
can smolder undetected for extended periods of time.

surface fire: Wildland fire that consumes dead material
above ground; the type most easily contained by
firefighting crews.

CHAPTER 22

HALFWAY THROUGH A sleepless night, I toss off my sheets, grab my spare set of keys for Jason's truck, and head for the drive-in coffee shack on the outside of town. There's always drip coffee at the base, but I'm going to need at least a triple shot before I face this day. All night, I've been agonizing over whether I'll be cut first thing in the morning, or whether Watters is mad at me, then cursing myself for even thinking like that—Watters is an instructor. I'm a candidate. That's that.

The drive calms me, and the quiet shuts up my brain, a little anyway. When I get back to base, I shower, letting the stream of water beat back the worst of my doubts, and suit up. They wouldn't really send me home because I got drunk on moonlight and lost my head for a second, would they?

I lace up for the morning run with shaking hands, ducking away from Jason's questioning looks. I *do not* want to talk about this. Griggs starts calling roll. I break into a sweat—why does my name have to be so far down the alphabet?

But it's there, along with the rest, as if nothing out of the ordinary happened. Watters stands shoulder to shoulder with Griggs, looking off into the distance, as usual, while he rattles off our names.

Maybe she didn't say anything?

Watters takes off when Griggs is done, and for once, I stay at the back of the pack—most of the way, anyhow. I sprint the last fifty yards so I finish in the top three—I'm not so off my game that I'd tank my scores. Not on purpose, anyway. When we return to the starting point, Watters peels away and doesn't look back.

I check my watch. Glucose is a little low, but that's to be expected after a run. I pop a few gummies and drain my canteen.

"Suit up!" Griggs hollers when the last recruit makes it back. "We're practicing jumps from the tower today with your reserve chutes and your PG bags attached so you can get a feeling for all ninety pounds of gear."

We hurry into our jumpsuits and follow him over to the tower. We already sat through classroom lessons about the aircraft, proper procedures for approaching, entering, and most important, exiting the aircraft. I know what to do, but knowing a thing and doing it aren't at all the same.

One by one, we file up into the tower, then wait in line as each jumper goes through their spotter check, clips in, and launches himself out the door. I fiddle with the straps across my chest, running my fingertips over the stitching that holds the clips in place. When it's my turn, the spotter—Griggs, of course—turns all his hawklike intensity on me.

"Are you ready?"

"Ready."

"Are you tight?"

"Yes."

"Hook up."

I clip my static line to the cable. He briefs me on the jump spot and conditions, and altitude. I suck in a breath. Just like jumping off the high dive at the pool back home, minus the water. I can't feel my hands. My feet are clumsy as blocks of wood. I look down—I have one hand clamped over my reserve chute, just like it should be. The other one is shaking like a rattlesnake's tail.

"Get in the door."

I drop to the floor and do a quick check of my gear.

"Turning final, three thousand feet. You are clear. Get ready."

A heartbeat later, Griggs bangs on my shoulder. Before I have time to think, I heave myself out the gaping hole in the metal. My stomach lurches. *Jump thousand, look thousand, reach thousand, wait thousand, pull thousand.* The cable catches my fall, jerking the line taut before I'm lowered like a rag doll down to the ground.

A giggle slips out when I feel the earth beneath me—*a giggle*. Like a five-year-old. My knees go all woozy and I sag against the line for a delirious moment. But not for too long—Griggs is shouting again.

"Unclip already! What's the holdup?"

Right. I stand on my own and release the cable.

Griggs leans out to grab the carabiner as it swings back to the open door. "Get back up here. You didn't grab your shins—your legs were jerking like a water skipper. You want a cannonball, Blair. Chin tucked, heels touching your butt."

"Got it."

"You will, yeah. Practice your jumps all the way back to the tower: six inches up, thirty-six inches out." With that, he ducks back inside to run through the spotter check again with a new jumper.

I hop like a rabbit back to the tower, no matter that I look like a complete idiot. Whatever—I'd hop clear to Bozeman if it means I make it through training and get to take that jump out of a real airplane.

The planet warms. Icebergs melt, seas rise, and hundred-year storm events sweep the landscape every twenty, ten, two years. Typhoons. Floods. Droughts. Ice storms.

And wildfires, which ought to be a cleansing force, burn too hot, too big to contain.

The planet warms, and it burns.

CHAPTER 23

TIME ON THE units ratchets up as we enter the middle stretch of training. The second day on the simulator, we practice overcoming problems in descent that might cause more of a crash landing than a properly executed PLF.

The day is nothing short of brutal. But every time one of us even looks like we might complain, Griggs howls something about this ground being like landing on a bunch of pillows compared to what we'll encounter *out there* and, yeah, he has a point, but that doesn't make it any easier to hear when you get a bunch of turf in your face mask or slam into the ground without enough bend in your legs.

The third time Yolo hits the dirt face-first and comes up shouting a string of curses, spitting sand out of his teeth, even Griggs has a hard time keeping a straight face. He releases us with a promise of more of the same over the coming days.

We pretty much grumble through the afternoon PT, then

do three laps around the two-mile circuit on the base. I'd take a ten-mile run in the forest any day over six miles running loops in the dirt in the training yard, but that's part of it—after the spectacle of jumping out of an airplane and parachuting back to earth, the actual work on a fire can be monotonous, and punishing. If you don't have the grit to cut line for ten hours on a fire and then get down on all fours to feel the dirt for hot spots with your bare hands, you don't have what it takes to do the job.

By the time the afternoon session is over, we're all a groaning, filthy mess. Just as we're hobbling toward the showers, we hear it—

The siren. It goes off with an earsplitting wail.

I grab Jason's arm. We both freeze, eyes on the tarmac and the sudden flurry of activity. The pilot and spotters head for the plane while ten jumpers run for the ready room to suit up. Two minutes later, they stride toward the aircraft, where they go through their buddy check, testing every strap and pin and buckle.

They load in one by one. The plane taxies, then rises into the air, banking and heading due north. It all happens so quickly—everybody knows their role and executes it with precision and focus. I shade my eyes, watching the plane as it grows smaller and smaller, the noise of the engine fading to nothing.

"That. Was. Awesome." Jason's grin splits his face.

"That's going to be us. *Weeks.* That's it, and then that's us up there." I can barely contain my excitement.

"Don't get ahead of yourself."

"I'm not! I mean it. I'm gonna be on that plane."

"Oookay." His grin reappears, even if it wobbles a little at the edges.

I drop my hand to my side and trot toward the dorms. I'm still sore and tired, and man, am I going to sleep well. But first I need to check my levels, log it all in my notebook, and then read through my notes on letdowns again, and gusty descents. My body will figure it out eventually, but I'll do even better if I can wrap my head around the steps first.

Nothing is going to stop me from getting up there, not if I can help it.

Fire Watch-Out Situations

No. 10: Attempting frontal assault on fire.

CHAPTER 24

THERE'S NOTHING LIKE jumping out of a plane for the first time.

That lurch in your belly. The way the force of your body plummeting through the air ripples the loose skin on your cheeks and tugs at your clothing. The way the whole world goes silent for a few delicious seconds while the earth spins beneath you.

After weeks of practice, on a bluebird day in mid-July, Griggs says we're ready. I step up to the open door of the aircraft while Hawkins calls out the last few spotter checks. My blood is roaring in my ears—I can barely hear his words even though he's shouting inches away from my face. I was so amped this morning, I could barely eat; now my stomach pitches and growls at me, furious.

I clamp a hand onto the red lever on my chest so the wind can't rip open my reserve chute. The engine roars, the wind howling in my ears as it rushes by.

Hawkins leans closer, hollering over the engine, "You are clear—"

I'm drowning in adrenaline, my legs weak as pool noodles. I sit in the door, feet dangling, the slipstream tugging at me, tempting me. The engine revs low.

"Get ready—"

Slap. All that training takes over and I hurl myself from the airplane. The wind yanks my body like a leaf and sends it tumbling. I pull the release and my parachute deploys, throwing my feet up to the horizon. The roar of sound stops and I drift through a bubble of silence. The whole world is a marble of swirling blue and green.

I check my canopy and airspace—all good. Then the controls—right turn, left turn, stall. My hands on the stays loosen. They're shaking. All of me is shaking—my torso convulsing in near-hysterical laughter. Adrenaline or joy or pure relief—I don't know and I don't care. Below, the canopy is lush and green, the sky above a dazzling cobalt blue. My body is weightless, a perfectly tuned instrument floating through it all.

As I near the landing spot, a ground wind batters me. Just as well—the last thing I need is for the guys waiting below to see me shaking and take it for weakness of some kind. I grit my teeth—I'm still moving fast—then I hit the ground and muscle memory takes over. I roll, absorbing the shock of impact.

I shoot to my feet in a tangle of line—I'll have to work on that part—fists clenched, knees bent. I let out a whoop so loud they probably heard it back at the base. The line of other trainees on the ground joins in, whistling and hollering.

I strip out of the padded jumpsuit, straighten the lines, and roll up my chute, packing it into my bag, then shoulder my gear and go join the rest to watch the sky. We stand shoulder to shoulder, waiting for the next guy to jump, counting the seconds under our breath until the parachute deploys, twisting reflexively as he nears the landing pad. I hold my breath as Norris hits the ground—he doesn't tuck and roll right, and *damn* that looked awkward. He comes up limping and cursing.

Griggs crosses the grassy field to have a look at the knee Norris is favoring. Once they are clear of the landing spot and Griggs is reassured the injury isn't anything serious, he lays into Norris about technique. The plane circles again, the sound of the engine changes, and we all look together toward the open door and the next jumper waiting for the slap on his shoulder.

It's Jason. I check my watch—my levels are fine. So why do I suddenly feel unsteady on my feet? In my head, I know Jason is every bit as well trained as me. He's done better on the simulator than I have. But still, watching his body hurtling through the air, it's all I can do to keep what little I had for breakfast in my stomach where it belongs.

The truth is—I'm responsible for him being here. If it weren't for me, he'd probably be playing football at a four-year university somewhere, safe and sound. If you ask, he'll deny that's what he'd rather be doing. I know he loves it out here, but—I don't think he had much of a choice in the matter, not with me for a best friend. It yanks at my insides on a normal day. And when he's doing something like plummeting through the air? It makes me want to puke.

Fortunately, I don't have long to worry. As soon as Jason comes into range, everybody on the ground can hear him hollering like a freaking cowboy. He lands, hopping up from the ground and pumping his fists in the air, a smile as big as his whole face, and I can breathe again. He comes at me, running, and sweeps me up in a bear hug—which is absolutely ridiculous since he's still in his bulky jumpsuit.

When the last rookie lands and rolls up his chute, Griggs waves everybody over. A few guys sit in the grass while the rest fan out in a semicircle behind them. I'm still far too amped to sit.

"This was just the beginning. We'll move you from flat, open, grassy fields like this to progressively steeper and more rugged terrain, smaller landing spots, and even a few emergency simulations to get you used to thinking quickly and problem-solving in the air."

Griggs sets one hand on his hip, the other propping the

clipboard where he can see it. "Let's iron out any sloppy technique before a tree takes off that flailing arm, Egan, or before failing to orient yourself into the wind on landing sends you face-first into a scree pile, Yolo."

Griggs rattles off critiques of everyone's form in his usual crisp manner. When it's my turn, I try to clamp down my goofy smile so he won't question if I'm taking his feedback seriously. But Griggs seems used to the sheen of spiking adrenaline rolling off us all—or maybe he isn't so far removed from his own rookie training that he's forgotten the thrill of a first jump.

I'm tired and bruised and so sore. But all I want is to get back up there again.

After dinner, I rap my knuckles against Jason's doorframe. The door is open, and he's sprawled on his back, a ball cap tipped over his eyes.

"I'm going for a run."

"After the day we've had?" He doesn't even bother flicking back the brim to look up. "You're nuts."

I shake out my legs, teasing the muscles loose. "I'm jittery. There's no way I'll sleep tonight if I don't run it out."

He groans. "Like I said, you're nuts."

I make my way outside, where I pause to adjust my trucker hat and give my quads and hammies a good stretch. I swing my arms across my chest and roll out my neck, breathing deep the cooling evening air.

Watters rounds the corner in her running gear and my arms slap to my sides, limp. For a second, I let myself imagine what it would feel like to fall into step beside her—just the two of us, with no pack breathing heavy on our necks. She glances my way, but her eyes skim right over me and she takes off without a second look.

I kick at the dust, then stretch my calves and hips, not because they feel like they need it—*I* need a minute. To calm down.

Yolo swings through the door then, nearly knocking into me. "Hey! You going for a run? Me, too."

I smirk. "I'll take it easy if you want to come along."

"Sure!"

"But I'm going to harp on you about your form the entire time."

He laughs. "Is it really that bad?"

"Yes."

"Right. Okay, then."

We take off at a jog across the parking lot. We've only gone a few steps when he speaks again. "You know, I could help you, too. I've got a degree in sports nutrition."

I stop, skidding out in the gravel. "What do you mean?"

Yolo rolls his eyes. "I've seen you portioning out your food and chomping down those energy chews all the time. And that day you got so dehydrated—come on, Blair. I know I seem like a goofball adrenaline junkie, but I do have a brain."

I let out a heavy breath. Is it that obvious? Has anyone else noticed?

"Hey, don't get mad—we all could use some help from time to time." At my glare, his hands fly up, defensive. "I'm not saying it's because you're a woman. No jumper is the best at everything, even the old guys who've been doing this for twenty years. That's why they attack those fires as a team. Everybody and every *body* is awesome at something; nobody's the best at everything."

I grunt and start jogging again.

"Asking for help when you need it isn't weakness. It's a different kind of strength."

I shake my head. Yolo doesn't get it—I can't afford to be anything *but* perfect. Griggs is looking for a reason to cut any one of us and send us packing. Anybody who thinks female candidates don't have to work twice as hard to prove themselves is ignorant or delusional, or both. And as a diabetic? Forget it.

"Another thing about the old guys around this place? They're pretty humble. Maybe they started out cocky as hell"—Yolo throws me a pointed look—"but the more I watch them, the more I start to think that's part of the job—the humble part, I mean."

Damn, he can talk. "Okay, okay. Enough yapping. I'm going

to forget that you just called me cocky and focus on the fact that you're going to crack your shins if you don't fix your heel strike."

That shuts him up. I start with his feet and work on his stride and posture up through the hips and core, then his shoulders and his chin. By the time we round out three miles, his face is creased with concentration, and he's finally stopped panting. And me? I've got to start being a lot more careful if Yolo—the most easygoing guy out here—has noticed there's something different about my relationship with food. But the jitters are gone from that nervy first jump, leaving me more tired than a short run should have any right to. I guess that's adrenaline, though—it revs you up, then knocks you flat once it's gone.

Base all actions on the current and expected behavior of the fire.

CHAPTER 25

THE SECOND JUMP is even better. When my feet hit the ground, I roll and pop up, resisting the urge this time to punch the sky like a high jumper who just smashed her personal record. I hurry to unclip, zip out of my jump gear, and stow it and my chute away. I have to hurry, because I got put in the last stick out of the plane today; everybody else is already gathered around Griggs and his damn clipboard.

I hustle over and plop onto the grass beside Jason, as far from Yolo as I can get. I can't tell if that guy's just trying to be nice or if he's the kind to rat me out to get ahead, so mostly I avoid him.

The second my butt hits the grass, Griggs starts in on his speech. "We intend to keep this training strictly to a four-week timeline so all of us are off active fire duty for the shortest stretch of time possible. I'd rather be out there jumping on fires like I was supposed to be doing right now, so none of you had better screw up your practice jumps and keep me grounded one day longer than is absolutely necessary. If that means we do two per day, that's what we'll do."

Jason and I exchange giddy smiles.

"Obviously, we can't control the weather, and we don't jump past certain benchmarks of high wind or visibility. So we have to make the most of good weather when we've got it."

Sure enough, we do two jumps the following day. The first is into a meadow just like the day before. The second is into another broad meadow, this time on a medium-size slope. My first landing is solid: arms in and feet together, and ending in a smooth, completed roll. But my second is—not great. The slope makes it seem like the ground is rushing at me twice as fast, and I hit hard, more like a belly flop than a controlled roll.

I stuff my gear into my bag, cursing, but it's hard to stay too down on myself when every time—every *single* time—Jason jumps out of a plane, he whoops and hollers the whole way down like a kid riding his first roller coaster.

Jason is all business once he gets to the ground, though— that's the job. Still, everybody's in good spirits when it comes time for Griggs to ream us for bad form on exit or landing, or anywhere in between.

We execute two more jumps the following day, into progressively smaller spots. And just because we're jumping doesn't mean the classroom sessions let up. Or the twice-a-day PT. Or the long-ass runs. We're all exhausted. I fall into bed every night with my eyes already fluttering closed, my body aching in places I didn't know it could. But I fall asleep happy, and wake up ready to get going. This is exactly where I want to be.

A few days later, on our eighth jump, into a strand of pebbles beside a wandering stream flanked by dense forest, Trout lands in a tree. He's the second-to-last one out of the airplane, so it's hard to say what happened; maybe the wind shifted and it wasn't his fault. Dirk, who jumps after him, narrowly misses the canopy, and if he hadn't tucked his legs up, a gnarly branch might have shattered his kneecap, no matter the pads there to protect it.

Griggs runs over to the tree, gesturing for the rest to follow so Trout can become a live object lesson. Griggs calls out instructions while Trout ties off, unclips, then slowly lowers himself using the letdown rope. We learned all this in the classroom already, and we practiced in the tower, but no matter how much you prepare for something, it's nothing like the real thing.

I enjoy the whole show more than I should—after Trout shoved my face into the sand on the O-course during hell week, I've been keeping my distance. I would have preferred to shove *his* face into something, but so far I've restrained myself. Pretty admirable, if you ask me. Now, as far as I'm concerned, the wind did the job for me; I didn't even have to get my hands dirty. I interlace my fingers behind my head, enjoying the view.

When Trout makes it to the ground, shaking and cursing, Griggs claps him on the back.

"See there? Aside from landing himself in a tree to begin with, Trout did everything right—he even dropped the canopy over the crown of the tree, not over a couple branches that are liable to snap when you're still thirty feet in the air. Good job." Trout gets another slap on the back. "Now, get up there and retrieve that expensive piece of taxpayer property."

While Trout steps out of his jumpsuit and into his harness and tree-climbing gear, still swearing, Griggs turns to face the rest of us, lecture-face ready.

"Depending on the urgency of the situation, and the rate of spread of the fire you've been tasked with putting out, you may have time to hustle up the tree and retrieve the chute when you land. Or, you may need to work on the fire for twenty-four hours and *then* have to climb the tree to get it down, which at that point, you'll be even more pissed at yourself for landing in the tree in the first place. But one way or another, that chute is coming down. You will not hike out without it."

By the end of Griggs's speech, Trout is climbing, and the second object lesson of the day begins, this time with more than a little snickering and jeering from those of us safely on the ground.

A wildfire can birth a tornado in its belly. It can boil a spring-fed stream down to nothing. It can shift the very earth, eating away at snaking underground roots, sending trees crashing to the forest floor and long-buried boulders tumbling downhill.

In an instant, fire can shift the ground beneath your feet.

CHAPTER 26

FOR OUR TENTH jump, I'm second to go in a three-person stick with Norris and Yolo. So much for avoiding Yolo. I'll just have to execute a flawless jump—then he'll have nothing to criticize, and nothing to be suspicious about. When the spotter sends down the streamers, we all watch as they drift sharply downward. My pulse speeds up, flaring in my fingertips—it's the tiniest jump spot we've done yet. Far below, shadows tip sidelong, a sure sign of a steep slope below and a tricky landing to come.

It's okay. I've got this.

The first stick is off, and we shuffle toward the back of the plane. Out the windows, through the grid on my face mask, I watch the first two jumpers fall, and mark the way they move in the air.

I've got this. Say it until you believe it.

The plane banks, circles back around, and then it's our turn. The spotter shouts instructions to Norris, then comes the *Get ready* and the slap on the shoulder. I get in the door, count down, then launch myself out of the aircraft. I plummet for a few weightless seconds before I deploy my chute and the whole sky is mine.

I tug at the toggles as I drift through the air—steering is finally becoming something like instinct. As I bear down on the landing spot, a shadow appears in my periphery. *What?* A gust of wind yanks at my feet, pulling me sideways. I checked my airspace—everything was clear. I jerk back around. The shadow is Norris—and he's way too close to me.

Either something went wrong with his chute or he hit a nasty gust of wind that blew him off course. I frantically steer away—tangling our lines would be the surest way to die from this height.

It works, and I veer away from Norris's flailing legs just in time. I check the ground beneath me—I'm going to miss the landing spot by a good ways. Suddenly, instead of hitting the tiny clearing the spotter indicated, I'm bearing down on a steep slope that's nothing but stumps. I grit my teeth, hoping the wind coming off the ground is strong enough to slow my approach. I tuck my knees higher than normal to avoid landing directly on a sheared-off stump, but I can't get them back down fast enough—I hit the ground hard and don't so much roll as crash onto my side.

I lie there, hissing short breaths—I can't seem to catch a full one.

"Blair!"

If I could breathe, I'd answer, but I can't seem to manage that yet.

"Blair! You okay?"

I try another breath, and it works, finally. I let my head loll back for a few delicious seconds, breathing. I blink, taking stock. I didn't hit my head—I know that much. I bend and flex my knees—all seems fine there. I can't do much with the guards over my ankles, but those joints don't seem to be the problem either. I test out my neck and my hip sockets—all good. A dislocated shoulder, maybe?

Something jabs at the soft skin of my belly. And something else is beeping—what is that? I rip off my left glove—*shit*. My watch face is shattered, an error message beeping loud enough to be heard in the clearing.

"Blair!" The voices are right on top of me now: Jason, Dirk, and Yolo hovering, and worried.

"Just give me a minute," I gasp, motioning them away.

Jason leans over and unclips the lines so Dirk can roll up my chute and pack it away. Free of the lines, Jason holds my elbow while I clamber to my feet.

"You okay?" Yolo's eyes are wide. "What's that beep—"

"I'm fine," I interrupt.

Jason's eyes go wide. "Come on." He throws me a glance that

reads *Bullshit, you're "fine."* But he herds Yolo and Dirk away, saying, "Blair just needs a minute. Let's give her some space."

Shit. That beeping doesn't sound anything like a radio or weather app. If Yolo wasn't suspicious before, he is now. I drop my head in my hands for a few seconds, breathing deep. Nothing I can do about that.

I zip out of my jumpsuit. Still hunched over, I pull up my shirt and peek beneath my waistband. The transmitter and sensor are intact, but my pump is dislodged and broken, hanging by a shred of medical tape, the broken half rattling around somewhere in my pant leg. Dammit. I'm going to have to guess my levels until we get back to base.

My brain turns painstakingly slowly. A broken watch—it's not great, but it's fixable. I can get a new one easy. But a broken insulin pump? That's *bad*. Aunt Cate's modifications void the warranty, so it could take weeks before the tech company and my insurance company get their shit together and send me a new one.

I struggle to my feet and walk slowly over to where the group waits for the last stick of jumpers to land. I'm moving slow, and it's more than just the pummeling that landing gave me. Jumper training is brutal. It takes everything a person has to make it through. And that's without diabetes.

My eyes burn. No. I am not doing the self-pity thing.

This was always going to be hard. It was always going to be

impossible. So what? Nothing has changed, not really. Across the clearing, Griggs bears down on Norris, his finger jammed into his chest.

"I told you there'd be no second chances for this class. You steer into another jumper and tangle the lines on a real fire, and not only do we have a containable lightning strike that spreads out of control, but we've got a couple of dead smokejumpers, too. Pack your bags when we get back to base and report to your old hotshot crew. They can use you; we can't."

Griggs turns away, looking for me. "You okay? That was one hell of an obstacle course you landed in."

I still have my helmet and face mask on, so if anything shows on my face, there's at least a crisscross pattern of metal and some well-placed shadows to hide it.

"Uh—I'll have Advil for dinner tonight and maybe soak in an ice bath for a bit. I'll be ready to go in the morning."

He nods. "Circle up!"

As Griggs rattles off notes for each of our jumps, the shock begins to wear off, and all that's left are the stiff and sore spots that'll be blooming black and blue soon. That, and a trail of worry winding through the dense forest of my thoughts. I'm *so* close. Without a working insulin pump, how am I going to make it through PT and practice on the units in that furnace of a jump-suit, not to mention five more jumps and the pack-outs that come with them, without my blood sugar spiking and sending me to the hospital?

"I can do this," I whisper.

But the words dissolve like ash on my tongue. Charred and bitter—that's what failure tastes like.

Fire Watch-Out Situations

No. 16: Getting frequent spot fires across line.

CHAPTER 27

AFTER GRIMACING THROUGH the evening meal, I borrow Jason's truck and drive into town, pulling into the first big-box store I spot. I pick up a smartwatch in the electronics department and an extra glucometer in the pharmacy just in case, along with a pack of alcohol swabs and a big bottle of ibuprofen, because every inch of me hurts.

In a dim corner of the parking lot, I dial Aunt Cate to fill her in. "So I'll have a second watch and a new pump sent directly to you? I can't risk somebody opening the box and seeing anything with the d-word on it."

"Sure, send them to me," she says. "But—are you sure you're okay?"

"Yeah, yeah. You know me." My voice cracks a little, but I just keep going. "You'll let me know when they're ready?"

"I will. But—I think it's time to tell your supervisors. From everything you've told me, you're doing great. Obviously, you've impressed them to get this far. Don't you think they'd want to know—to support you? I worry about you."

She has a point. Still—what if she's wrong and I get kicked out? That's the one thing I *can't* handle. "No way. But I'm being smart. I promise."

I hear a heavy sigh on the other end.

"You're really going to give yourself a shot every morning and another one at every meal? And you're going to keep those needles and injection sites clean in the field how, exactly?"

"We practiced for this, remember?"

"For an emergency, yes. This is not—"

"Fessing up is as good as quitting and you know I can't do that."

"It's too dangerous! Blair. Come on. Think about the consequences if something goes wrong: organ failure, blindness, amputation, coma. We agreed on a calculated level of risk; what you're talking about blows right past that."

I let out a quavering sigh. "I'll check in with an endocrinologist when I graduate. Okay?"

There's a long silence. "Until then, you won't be in the field overnight?"

"Shouldn't be."

"You'll use a glucometer to test your levels every morning and evening, and in between when you're able?"

"Yes."

"And you have enough of the long-acting and rapid-acting shots to last two weeks?"

"Four. I've been storing up."

Aunt Cate sighs. "I don't like it. I'm not promising I won't call the base and give them an earful. But I will get to work on your pump and watch the minute they arrive."

"Thank you." My eyelids flutter shut. I'm exhausted, and the hard part is just beginning. "I can handle this, you know."

"I know you can—you're tough as hell and damn smart. But you don't know when to walk away—you never have."

Aunt Cate's worry rings in my ears all the way back to the base. Inside my room, I make myself as comfortable as I can lying on a bunch of strategically placed ice packs. I peel down my sweatpants and jab a new sensor into my abdomen, then click in my one spare transmitter. I close my eyes for a minute while the app that will then link the transmitter to my new smartwatch downloads. I can't fault Aunt Cate—it's risky not having the insulin pump to continuously regulate my levels in the field. But what choice do I have?

I comb through my supplies, bagging daily insulin doses and checking the logs in my notebook. I could bring the glucometer in the field—that would be the safest thing. But it's risky enough hiding insulin in my bag—if somebody sees, it's over. Yolo already knows something's up. Maybe he wouldn't report me, but I can't take that risk.

Jason tiptoes in before long, his ukulele tucked under one arm and his brow furrowed with concern. When he opens his mouth to say something, I cut him off.

"Don't," I whisper. "Please."

So he sits on the end of the bed and strums quietly. The worry doesn't leave his face, but at least he pretends not to notice the tears of frustration leaking out of my eyes.

The ponderosa pine is a fascinating creature.

When flames lick the understory, a mature tree's branches are well out of reach of even the tallest flames. If fire bites into the thick bark and takes hold, the tree sloughs off flaming chunks of its own skin, saving the canopy, and with it, the whole forest.

The older a tree gets, the more fire-hardy it becomes. But even the mighty ponderosa can't survive a crown fire.

CHAPTER 28

FIRST THING THE next morning, Griggs drives us into the woods for another crosscut-saw lesson. I close my eyes and tilt the brim of my hat down over my face on the way there, pretending to be asleep. Yolo keeps trying to catch my eye, but I am not in the mood to talk.

Griggs marches us fifty yards into the woods, sets up beside a gorgeous old-growth ponderosa, and leans the saw against the tree like he's going to lecture us on proper care and cleaning of our tools *again*. Instead, he folds his arms over his chest. "Never mind the saw."

What? Jason and I exchange a look. Griggs is messing with us.

"When you're in the field and the fire is out, you have to pack every ounce of gear back out with you. Sometimes it's a quick five-mile hike. Other times it's up half a mountain and the better part of a day before you get to somewhere we can reach you."

Griggs claps his hands together. "We need to know you can

handle a long, tough hike with a heavy pack, in unmarked territory. So let's go."

I turn around, cursing my dumb luck. Before the accident, I would have crushed a pack test—especially when there's orienteering involved. Now, to keep my levels steady, I'm going to have to go at a maddeningly slow pace.

Jason jogs to catch up, then leans in and speaks in a low voice: "It is not smart for you to be out on a long hike in the middle of nowhere without a pump."

"So, what? I should just quit now? Is that what you're saying?"

His voice ratchets up an octave. "Come on, Blair. You could spike. You could overheat. You could get dehydrated again, easily."

"I won't. Stop overreacting."

Jason rakes a hand through his hair. "What about me? So you don't care what happens to you—whatever. When you go into a diabetic coma because you've got a hundred pounds on your back and you're in the middle of the wilderness where no one can get to you in time—that's a shitty thing to do to your best friend."

"I'll be fine. Just—I just need you to cover for me."

"And what if I don't want to anymore?"

"*Jason.*"

"I'm sick of covering for you. So you can prove what, exactly? Anybody who really matters can see how great you are at this.

If they don't, that's their problem. When are you going to stop caring if one person out of a thousand doubts you? They don't matter. *You* do."

"Look." I drop my voice—the others are getting close to the trucks. "You don't get it. People don't doubt you by default, then see if you can convince them otherwise. I can't afford for Griggs or Hawkins or anyone else to second-guess my abilities—not when I'm this close. I know you're only trying to keep me safe, but I can't stop now. I *have* to do this."

The others have begun leaping in and out of the truck beds to collect a pack, shoulder it, and adjust the straps for the added weight. Jason jams his hands on his hips. Yolo is up in the bed of the truck, dragging one of the packs to the edge.

"Hey, Yolo, grab me one?" I ask.

He props the one he picked out for himself on the tailgate, and while he's still holding on, I slide my arms through the straps and cinch them down. When Yolo lets go, I clip the belt over my hip bones, then pull the straps tight. I stay like that, the pack's weight resting on the tailgate, while Griggs briefs us—doing anything I can to cut corners and save my energy.

"This isn't a timed test; you just have to find your way back to the pickup point. This is not a group exercise; we'll stagger your start times so you're out there on your own. If you help another candidate find their way, you both fail. You each have radios in your pack, so if you get in trouble, call it in and we'll come get you."

Jason shoots me a look.

Griggs slaps the stack of maps in his hand. "So who wants the first slot? Let me guess—Blair?"

"Yep." I take the map and compass Griggs offers and flash what I hope is an indifferent smile.

"I'll give you all a hint." Griggs points west. "Start that way."

I take off, getting my bearings while I walk. Two dots are inked on the map: the red one where we were dropped and the blue one which will be our pickup point. I know the running routes on the outskirts of town pretty well, and though I've never come out this way, I have a good idea of our location. I've got two choices to make it to the blue dot: steeper and shorter, or flat but long. The long way looks to be about fourteen miles, the short way more like eight. The pack has a full canteen strapped to each hip, and probably more on the inside. And I have plenty of gummies stashed in my pockets. I can do this. I just have to be smart. And patient—that will be the tricky part.

I pick the long way—go as fast as I can when the terrain allows, to get as far as I can before the sun rises to its highest, hottest point. I take it slow and steady on the climbs, pausing in the shade to breathe, no matter that my brain is screaming at me that if I don't hurry, I'll finish last. The old wildland adage *Ounces equal pounds and pounds equal pain* has never been more true, and I want to punch the guy who first thought up that gem. If I make it through this without getting cut, I'm going to comb through every item in my pack and try to cut weight when I get back to the dorms—I don't have a choice at this point.

The forest is quiet, and with as busy as my mind is, it's a respite of sorts to hear nothing but birdsong and squirrels scrabbling up the tree trunks to get out of my way. I take a sip of water every five minutes. I nibble off a corner of a chew every ten. I check the readout on my watch every fifteen. Slow and steady. I can do this.

I stop for lunch where I can rest my feet in a passing stream to cool my core temperature. I stick a shot of long-acting insulin into my thigh while I force myself to breathe and eat slowly. I peel away the bread from my pastrami sandwich and leave the crackers unopened—those simple carbs are easy enough for the insulin pump to correct for, but I can't afford that kind of spike now. I polish off everything else in the bag even though I don't feel one bit hungry.

Whatever. I can manage a hike with a heavy pack without passing out. What I can't handle is making it through hell week, ten successful jumps, and then washing out because of a stump.

I'm not the first to make it to the truck, but I'm not the last either. Any other day it would have burned to land in the bottom for a strength and orienteering test. But all I can think about is what my numbers will be when I finally make it back to my room, jab myself with a needle, and see what the glucometer says.

Watters, who's been avoiding me ever since that night in Operations, watches through narrowed eyes as I plod slowly to the truck. I ignore her, and brush aside Jason's offered hand.

"Come on, let me help you," he whispers.

I grit my teeth, ignoring the look on his face, and clamber into the truck bed alone.

That night, Jason brings my dinner to my dorm room, and he takes notes while I prick myself and make some calculations. He even drives to the big-box store to grab some juice boxes like I'm a five-year-old or something. Then he plunks himself at the end of my bed and yammers, yodels, anything he can do to distract me. Eventually, my levels even out; I don't remember him leaving.

By the end of the week, we get in our last few training jumps. I'm careful to save my pee breaks for a time when I feel myself getting lightheaded, or when I know I've been sweating too much, so I can prick myself and get a quick reading. I stop eating with the guys—I take my food to my room where I can be alone and think, and suck down a juice box if I need to. Still, stress is showing through the cracks. Dark smudges make camp under my eyes and don't show any sign of leaving.

Watters is suddenly paying attention to me again, and not for any of the reasons I might want. Jason hovers like an anxious nurse. Nobody else seems to notice—okay, maybe Yolo. But all of us are breaking down in one way or another. Some of the guys have dropped too much weight. Others nurse old injuries or hot spots that threaten to turn into nasty blisters. Everybody's dealing with something. Everybody's hiding something. At least, that's what I tell myself.

Post lookouts when there is possible danger.

STANDARD FIREFIGHTING ORDERS, NO. 5

CHAPTER 29

ON A HAZY July morning, Hawkins gathers the thirteen of us left. Watters stands over his left shoulder; Griggs waits over his right. Instead of rattling off a list of training exercises for the day, he speaks in a different tone, less like a drill sergeant, more like a crew boss.

"I'll be damned. I did not think I'd see so many of you standing here at the end of training. I definitely did not think there would be teenagers in any class of jumpers that graduated under my watch. But you've done yourselves and this base proud."

Graduated? All around me, the guys shift their feet—glancing around, confusion twitching and tugging into relieved smiles.

So it's over? We made it?

"Don't get any ideas. You are at the very bottom rung of the ladder. Hell, you've still got both feet on the ground, looking up. You may spend the rest of this season tending gear and pulling weeds. If you do jump, it will be paired up with a veteran, and out on tiny lightning strikes that really only need a little dirt shoveled over the bits of duff that are smoldering, with a long, boring hike out. Do not expect to see time on any big fires this season. As far as I'm concerned, you're all still rookies until you prove otherwise."

I sneak a glance at Jason. He's got this wobbly, nervous smile I don't think I've ever seen on him before. When he catches me looking, a laugh bubbles up from deep in his chest. He manages to keep it mostly silent, but his shoulders are shaking with incredulous, ridiculous laughter.

Griggs walks down the line, placing a pin into each of our upturned palms.

And just like that, I'm a smokejumper.

Hawkins clears his throat. "I'll be calling you into my office this morning for placements. As of this moment, this base is no longer a training facility. We'll still keep a close eye on you rookies who are stationed here, but this base is now back to full-time support for fire-suppression efforts across the region. If you're the praying sort, ask for an early fall and a long, hard winter so we can regroup, lick our wounds, and replenish our numbers by next spring."

A call comes in a few hours later. The siren goes off and the jumpers stationed at the base spring into action. Jason and I leave our gear on the table and jog to the door to watch the pros in action.

Both Watters and Griggs are among those suiting up and running to the plane. After being grounded for weeks, critiquing technique and drilling us in every aspect of the job, they're like a pair of wild animals who only pretended to be tame for a while. They bump fists, sharing an eager grin before they step into the plane. In a matter of minutes, the aircraft is in the air and a crew of six jumpers is off to fight the fire.

"Whoa."

"Yeah," I breathe. "Our turn is coming up. Soon."

Jason glances my way. "I can't decide whether I'm more terrified or excited."

"Isn't that the same thing?"

"For you, maybe," he says.

Details trickle in from Operations as the hum of the plane's engines fades. What was probably a cigarette butt tossed out the window of a passing car in the Sawtooth Range started a small fire. It would have taken hours for handcrews to get up there by road, so jumpers were called in. Luckily, a nearby lookout saw the smoke and got started fighting the fire on one flank with a jury-rigged pump drawing water out of a creek. Because there's a road leading to the lookout tower, that load of jumpers will get a ride home in a truck tonight, once the fire is out, without having to pack out their gear—a rare luxury they'll be crowing over once they get home.

While I'm still watching the spot where we lost sight of the plane, Hawkins calls five of us into his office to announce that we'll be joining his crew. I glance around the room. Yolo and Dirk, plus Jason, me, and Luís—the only other teen who didn't wash out. Seems like Hawkins wants to keep the three of us close. Just because we didn't give him any reason to cut us during training doesn't mean he can't throw any one of us off the base whenever he wants. I guess training never ended.

Fine. People have been underestimating me my entire life. Proving them wrong is nothing new.

The sound of a friendly campfire—the crackle and hiss of the flames, the wheeze of air rushing through gaps in the coals, pockets of pitch popping—it's balm to a weary soul. Comforting; mesmerizing, even. But when the whole forest is on fire, the sound of all that fuel burning up at once is a primal roar. The onslaught of noise dulls the senses, raising the hiss of nerves to a frenzy.

A forest on fire is fury that's found its earthly form.

CHAPTER 30

AFTER WE FINISH our work in the gear room, eat lunch, and get our PT done for the day—on our own schedule for once—Jason calls me over to his truck. "Come on, let's celebrate. You and me."

"Cheeseburgers? Steak? Fried chicken? Whatever—I don't care. Let's go."

We drive into town, windows down, the radio turned all the way up. Jason drums on the steering wheel and sings while I douse my cheeks in the wind.

"Can you believe it?" I say in a break between songs. "We're smokejumpers!"

He laughs. "I called my mom right after Hawkins told us. She hates it *so* much."

Yeah. "I'm sure she blames me."

"Nah. She just wishes I was bashing my brains in for some college football team. She doesn't get that making it through jumper training is like playing in the major leagues or being a navy seal or . . . I don't know." He pauses, his hands going still. "She wants me to have a regular life."

"Sure." Isn't that what most parents want—for their kids to be successful at something they understand? And to be safe. Most parents don't dream of their kids jumping out of planes.

I know he won't be a jumper forever—he'll end up with some respectable job in an office or office-adjacent; when Janie finishes medical school they'll have a bunch of kids and live that normal, suburban life his mom wants for him. Maybe that's what draws him out here, to the craziest job on the planet. Maybe he's getting the wild out of his system. Or maybe it's a casualty of being best friends with me—I love this so much he never had any choice but to love it, too.

But me? I never could see far enough into the future to even imagine normal. Now that I'm here—now that I landed the job I dreamed of my whole life—I'm never leaving.

So let's celebrate already. "Where are we headed? Putt-Putt golf? The pizza parlor? Food trucks?"

He wriggles his eyebrows. "Even better."

Jason spins the wheel with his palm and pulls into the parking lot of a beige medical office building. He throws the truck into park and yanks the key out of the ignition. "'I'll check in with an endocrinologist when we graduate.' Your words, not mine."

I set my teeth. "Aunt Cate ratted me out."

"Yep."

"But—we'll be waiting all afternoon for them to fit us in. And most GPs don't know much about type one. Come on, this is a waste of time."

"That was my second call this morning. The specialist is expecting you." He shrugs, like it's out of his hands.

I let out a shaky breath. Back in high school, I'd prep for *days* before a track meet, lying in bed, visualizing pillowy landings, perfectly timed handoffs, and podiums with me at the top. I prefer to handle endocrinologist visits the same way, mentally preparing for bad news and sterile rooms crowded with disapproving adults. Heights don't scare me. Wildfire doesn't scare me. But my body betraying me again?

That's flat-out terrifying.

Besides, I've always been careful to have my annual physicals done at some rural clinic with no access to any of my damning medical records from the big hospital systems in Colorado. Thanks to this visit, my diabetes will be on record in Montana for the first time. Now where am I going to find a doctor who will sign off on my medical release each year—Alaska?

"I know you hate this." Jason throws his door open. "If it was anything less than your life on the line, I wouldn't push."

I sigh, but follow him inside. "We've really got to talk about your idea of *celebrating.*"

He grins. "Plenty of time for that at the pizza parlor."

. . .

Twenty minutes later, I'm dressed in one of those oversized gowns that always seem to be gusting open at the wrong moments, while the intake nurse takes blood samples then asks a barrage of questions, scowling every time he doesn't approve of my answer. When that's done, he shows me into an office; a few minutes later, a knock sounds on the door and the endocrinologist shows herself in. She sits in front of the computer, clicking through my chart.

"You were diagnosed two years ago, at seventeen?"

"Yeah."

"And your pump broke how?"

"I landed wrong on a stump."

She sends me a withering look. "A stump. How long ago was this?"

"Um, I guess eight days."

The doctor screws up her lips. "And you waited that long to come in because . . . ?"

"I was regulating it on my own."

"I see. As I'm sure you know, the greater your activity level, the more critical and precise the measurements need to be." She gestures at the musculature in my arms. "You're clearly an athlete."

"Uh-huh."

A tight sigh, and another look. "If you can't be compelled to take care of yourself for health reasons, maybe you'll listen because of performance. If you send yourself into shock, you'll set yourself back significantly in whatever fitness goals you have."

The nurse raps on the door, then hands the endocrinologist a series of printouts. She tips her glasses down on her nose and spreads the papers along the exam table. I fix my gaze on my hands. I don't want to look, not if it's bad.

"And how high was your top reading last week?"

"Two hundred fifty."

"And your lowest?"

"Sixty."

Her brow furrows.

I sigh, whip out the notebook I use to log my readings, and hand it over. I hate hospitals, medical offices, fancy clinics—all of it. That chemical aftertaste on the air. The buzz of machines. A staticky silence stretches out while she pages slowly through the notebook.

Yeah. She's not impressed.

"As it is, I'd advise a complete halt in activity until we get a week of consistent readings along acceptable levels."

My gaze slides to the calendar on the wall. We're in the middle of the worst fire season the West has seen in recent memory. They need every able body out there containing those fires, and

Hawkins is clearly watching us rookies for signs of weakness. I can't afford to be benched.

"Sure, I can definitely do that in a month or so."

The doctor's eyebrows climb. "And why is that?"

"For . . . professional reasons."

"I'd strongly advise against a strenuous career that will put your health at risk. It isn't sustainable. And episodes like this where you aren't able to properly monitor your levels could have serious long-term consequences."

I don't answer. This isn't the first time a doctor has told me that the only career I want is out of the question.

"What kind of activity are we talking about?" she asks.

"Oh, you know, hiking, gardening, some cross-training. Jogging."

The doctor gives me a hard look; when no further explanation comes, she sighs again. Her fingers clatter across the keyboard, submitting a request for the replacement pump I so badly need.

When I make it back to the truck, Jason has his hat tilted to cover his eyes and his head resting on the seat back. That guy can sleep anywhere. I scoot into my side and slam the door shut.

He shoots upright, rubbing his eyes. "Well?"

"A shiny new pump on order. *Finally*."

Jason rolls his eyes. "And?"

"And what?"

"And she didn't say anything about the health risks?"

"Come on, Jason."

"*You* come on. You told that specialist you're a smokejumper and she said, 'Sure, go ahead and keep throwing yourself out of planes and working sixteen-hour shifts with limited rations out there in the heat and smoke'? 'With or without a working insulin pump'?"

"Well, no. But she knows I'm an athlete."

"Blair!"

"I'll be *fine*."

Jason snatches the paperwork out of my hand and scans the fine print. "You can't still plan to jump with numbers like this. Seriously, Blair?"

"I'll take it easy. I'll stop training on my off days."

He shakes his head. "I don't understand why you're doing this. I don't know why you think you still have anything to prove to anybody."

"Jason—I haven't even jumped one fire. I passed rookie training, sure, but you heard Hawkins. To him, and probably to half of the veterans on base, we're a bunch of kids who never should have come within spitting distance of training camp to begin with. The only way to convince them otherwise is to prove it, out there, on a fire."

"And once you do that, then you'll stop? Or will you find some other excuse to keep pushing yourself past your body's limit?"

"The doctor said my numbers will stabilize—in a matter of weeks. And there's not much more than that left in the season. So I'll tough it out for a while longer. Then I can rest and reset once the snow puts out the last of the wildfires."

His face is all hard lines. "I don't like it."

"I know. But I'll be fine, really. I can handle this."

He rubs his hands over his face. He doesn't respond.

"Now, where's my celebration? I haven't had a steak in weeks. No—I want a whole platter of bacon-wrapped shrimp. No—"

Jason sighs and lets out a reluctant smile. "Let's just get everything on the menu and eat until we can't stand up." Then he cranks up the music and backs out of the parking lot. "Well, *I* will, anyway. You get to eat your allotted carb intake and not a crumb more."

"Yeah, yeah."

While Jason's attention is on the road, I sneak a look at his face. He's worried, that's obvious. And I get it—I know I can't keep this up forever. But I'm not going to take two weeks to rest before I even get started. They'll have to bench me before I say no to jumping on every single fire I can this summer.

Fire Watch-Out Situations

No. 13: On a hillside where rolling material can ignite fuel below.

CHAPTER 31

I'M RESTLESS THE whole next day. My body itches to go for a run—a long one. But I promised Jason I'd rest when I could. If I want to get him off my back and believe I'm taking this seriously, I need to follow through. Plus, I have a hard time convincing even myself that risking a dip in blood sugar to feed a runner's high is a good idea.

Instead, I settle beside Jason where he sprawls in the row of chairs opposite the jump list. Over the course of training, the dorms cleared out as candidates washed and were sent packing. And now that half of the graduating class has been sent to other bases and so many jumpers are still deployed to the south, the place feels like a ghost town.

It isn't lonely, though. Watters and Griggs are stationed in Missoula, and I got to know Aloha, one of the other veterans on base, when he stepped in as spotter for our last few training jumps. And there are two other women on base, even if they don't live in the dorms: a pilot named Deb, and Lois, a no-nonsense dispatcher. Anyway, I could never really be lonely, not with Jason around.

He glares at the jump list, his legs stretching across the empty space.

"At least we're not at the bottom," I offer.

He snorts. "That other name beneath ours is the old guy who runs the copy machine and keeps the coffee percolator going. He's retiring at the end of the month and I heard he hasn't jumped in years. They keep his name there as a last resort—and so they don't have to demote him."

"Humph."

There are only two dozen jumpers at the base, so there's a chance we'll get called soon. But it isn't likely. Jason digs into his shirt pocket for a Gin Gin. He tears open the packaging and bites down, his jaw clicking as he chews through candy as sticky as pine resin.

"I'd offer you one, but . . ."

I throw him a look. "Haven't you heard—I'm *very* concerned about my health."

Jason drops his head back, laughing.

"Janie still sending you care packages?"

"Every week." He continues to work his jaw, trying not to yank out a tooth.

"If you're not going to lock that down, you've got to cut her loose, J. Put her out of her misery."

"And give up the only way to get Gin Gins out here? Not a chance."

But it's more than that. Technically they are off-again—she's dating somebody else and of course there are plenty of women in town who'd be happy to keep Jason company. But it's always been Janie for him, and I'm betting it always will be.

The next fire call comes three days later. It's only a two-stick jump, so a four-person crew—no need for me and Jason. Instead, we're sent out to supervise a thinning operation.

The silver lining? Well, there are two. First, it's way easier to keep a steady blood sugar level if I'm "supervising" rather than working a fire line, so I get to count that as a rest day. Second, by the time I get back to base, my name is four spots higher on the jump list.

I've never been any good at taking it easy.

Fight fire aggressively,
having provided for safety first.

STANDARD FIREFIGHTING ORDERS, NO. 10

CHAPTER 32

AT 1500 HOURS, the siren goes off. I'm eighth on the list and Jason is seventh, meaning we're both going up this time. I swear, my heart stutters to a stop, then restarts with a kick of adrenaline that sizzles through my whole body. My chute is packed, and my gear. My sensor and transmitter are good to go, and I've got my insulin doses packed. All I have to do is suit up and get on that plane. I set off at a run.

When I exit the ready room, there's Yolo, grinning down at me, ready for the buddy check.

"You are jumping a square."

"Yup."

He squats to touch each strap and clip as he checks all the way from the stirrups under my boot to the AAD. "Did you do a self-test?"

"Yes."

"Did you check your reserve knife?"

"Yes." Only a dozen times.

Chest strap, cutaway handle, drogue—we've both got each prompt memorized by now. Yolo hands me a static line clip. "Do you have a helmet, gloves, and letdown rope?"

"Yep!"

Yolo slaps me on both shoulders. "Good flight."

I return his grin, my belly beginning to churn with that cocktail of excitement and dread. "You're not jealous?"

"Nah—we're a team. Today, I'm here for you."

I load into the plane, shaking my head. Jason and I are a team, sure. The other rookies? Maybe someday. Yolo's all right, and Dirk. But the whole crew—on my team? I highly doubt that. Last season I made friends with guys I thought had my back. But no—I learned the hard way that the bros had each other's backs, not mine.

Except Jason. He and I are a team. I don't need anyone else.

I sit beside Griggs—my jump partner. Apparently, I'll never get out from under that guy's nose. Whatever—I'm here. I'm finally here!

Griggs takes one look at my face and rolls his eyes. "Either you quit grinning like a maniac or nobody's going to want you on their crew. Only the psychos get that evil look in their eye before a jump."

I bite down on my upper lip, not that it has much effect on the rest of my face. Jason sits opposite me, paired with Watters. He flashes a thumbs-up and I let my grin back out for a second. This is it—what we trained for all summer. No—more than that. I've been waiting for this my entire life.

The plane takes off and within minutes we're over the wilderness. The spotter passes along details about the fire. An afternoon thunderstorm sent up a plume of smoke in the Flathead Range. If the fire runs to the west, it should hit a line of peaks and fizzle out. If it runs north, it could roll all the way to the Canadian border. Our job is to get to the fire before it has that chance.

I watch out the window, studying the ripples and bends in the topography. When Aunt Cate used to drive us way back into the woods for a hunting or fishing trip, I'd lie awake in my bivvy at night, staring up at the Milky Way against that midnight blue, the ragged tops of the trees framing the clearing where we'd set up camp, and think we must be the only two human beings to ever set foot on that particular pad of dirt, at least in the past hundred years.

Jumping into a fire in the middle of nowhere has that same feeling, like you've zipped back through time to land on a square of untouched earth. There's something sacred about land that has never seen a power line or road, where the only sign of civilization is an occasional airplane leaving a white trail across the sky.

After about ten minutes, the spotter lifts one hand to his

headset while he takes instructions from the base about wind speed, temperature ratings, and the rest, leaning out to get a better look at the fire.

Griggs shouts above the roar of the engine, "You do not want to miss your landing. This is not forgiving terrain."

No shit. The forest from above is a different thing altogether—the way the trees change shape as you pass over them, a million skinny green cones wriggling beneath you. The plane banks left, and there's our landing spot—an open grassy area, and over the ridge beside it, a thread of smoke rising from the canyon to spread out among the clouds. The plane banks again, and the spotter tosses paper streamers out the door. I trace their downward path, watching the wind as it tugs them toward the meadow.

The first stick, with Aloha as the JIC and Luís, steps up to the door. The spotter shouts the final check while the wind plucks at their suits, beckoning. A slap on the back, and Aloha is out. A pause, and then Luís is gone, too. Jason and Watters are next, and before long, they're flying. When Griggs steps into line, I shuffle beside him. The plane hits a pocket of air and we pitch to the side, straining to stay upright—no easy thing when you're standing in ninety pounds of gear.

Griggs leans over and shouts into my ear, "Keep your distance while we're in the air and we'll meet up on the ground."

"Got it!"

He nods and steps up to the open doorway. I know the spotter is shouting instructions, but I can't process a thing with excitement jamming my ears and restless energy coursing through me. *Slap*—out goes Griggs. My stomach sinks clear to my toes. I sit in the open door, fix my eyes on the horizon, and launch myself into the air.

Jump thousand.

Look thousand.

Reach thousand.

Wait thousand.

Pull thousand.

Whoosh.

Silence.

Total and complete silence.

For a moment, I let myself glory in the sky above, and the horizon stretching out beyond, let that sweet peace roll over me. Then I get to work. My hands on the steering guides, I maneuver my chute with a tug on the left, then the right, then the left again as the jump spot nears. My toes skim what feels like inches above the top of the canopy before the ground is speeding toward me and I twist to turn myself to face the wind. I bite down hard on my mouthguard, pumping my breath through gritted teeth. At the last minute, my hips swing around and, feet together, I hit the ground and roll onto my side, then onto my back, my feet kicking up over my head.

No sooner than I land, my head snaps up and I glance around the clearing. There are Griggs and Watters and—a long breath whooshes out of me—Jason, on his feet and resolutely packing his chute into his bag. I unclip, stepping out of my landing gear to do the same. The last stick is about to land, while the first pair of jumpers have their eyes on the sky, waiting for the gear boxes to drop into the clearing one after another. No sooner than they land, the guys pry them open and start setting up camp.

I stash my food into my pack, then cinch everything down so I'm ready to work. The sky is still blue—the smoke hasn't smothered it yet. And the air is clear. I can only catch a faint whiff of the fire. The trees up here are thin—a good sign for us.

The fire is small so far, though what will happen in the next twenty-four hours is anybody's guess. Better to be prepared for the worst. By the time I strap on my gear, check my radio, and heft my Pulaski for the hike into the fire, the eight-person crew is already collecting at the far edge of the clearing, ready to go. It's all happened in a matter of minutes.

I flash Jason a smile as I step into line. We don't run up the ridge between us and the fire, but it's close. All that nervous energy from the jump has to go somewhere, and if there's any time to hurry up, it's now, before the fire has a chance to start spreading.

We get to the top and look down. Aloha calls out the exit routes and splits us into two groups, sending us down into the meadow below to see if we can pinch off the head before the fire reaches the bottom of the next ridge over.

I follow Griggs and Aloha straight downhill. It's steep going—more like controlled falling than hiking as our boots skid sideways for grip. We stop at the rock outcropping that will anchor our line. Griggs fires up the chainsaw and starts hacking at the brush and toppling trees, while Aloha and I take turns clearing the slash and chucking it well clear of the line, or hacking at the ground, digging a fire line away from the base of the ridge. Luís stays on the outcropping, serving as the lookout.

I ran track long enough to understand that mastering some distances is about setting a pace, sticking to it, and learning how to get your brain to shut up about how much your legs hurt. Other distances are flat-out all-out, about breath and fight and the fiercest sprint you can summon. Digging a fire line in the middle of the wilderness with no rescue on its way to lift you out of there is a nasty combination of both: a full-out sprint that lasts for hours. Nothing less will get the job done. So I manage my breath, shut up my brain, and check over my shoulder to gauge the fire spread.

Once we've constructed a solid line around the meadow and begun to loop up the ridge along the east flank, we stop for a water break and take stock. I gnaw on my gummies and, between deep breaths and long drags of water, run through a quick calculation of hours of exertion and likely calories burned versus water, carbohydrate, and electrolyte intake. I check my watch for my sensor's readings. Yep. All clear—for now.

I crank the lid back onto my canteen, scanning the terrain. Between where we stand and the anchor point, the ground is a smoking, charred mess, but the flames are gone. We'll have a hell of a job mopping up still, but that'll have to wait. All eyes on the ridgeline above us, Aloha lifts the radio to his ash-smeared face.

"Watters, Aloha." The fire is racing upward, eating up land twice as fast as the other crew can move.

A crackle, and then, "This is Watters. Go."

"We're going to circle around through the black and help you button up that side."

"Good. Watch yourselves."

"Copy that."

Griggs and I shoulder our tools and take off, straight into the smoldering dirt. We scramble up the ridge until we're nipping at the heels of ten-foot-high flames licking upward scary fast. We slow to a brisk hike and circle around the backside. It's scree on the other side of the ridge—a stroke of luck, finally. We slot our tools onto our packs, using both hands to scramble across. At the top of the ridge, the sun breaks through, soft where it hits the rising cloud of smoke, and in the gaps between smoke, shafting through the trees in a circular burst of white.

The fire will have a harder time rolling over the ridge in that spot, with nothing for fuel for at least thirty feet. But if those trees at the top of the ridge catch fire and topple over, sending embers or flaming pinecones rolling down the hill, then it's over—there'll be no way for our small crew to contain the fire.

When we reach the west side, Griggs fires up the chainsaw and sets to toppling the stand of evergreens near the top of the ridge, and Aloha and I head to meet the others, where they rush to pinch off the last section near the top. They only have a few dozen yards to go to seal off that flank, but the flames are within spitting range. The fire is traveling in leaps and spurts—unlike a grass fire where the burn is a single thread of fire, in brush and forest, brambles and bushes toss the flame forward, skipping and leaping with every burst of wind.

I hack away at the earth a few steps behind Aloha, first with a swinging chop, then a flick that tosses the dirt up in chunks. And because I'm not part of a twenty-person fire line, I go back and chop again and again, tossing until my own line is deep and wide. No way am I going to let any section I touched be the spot where the fire breaks through.

People who've never seen jumpers in action don't understand the hype. It's assumed they're arrogant, that their egos far outpace their abilities, and that they're the same as anyone else, only with the adrenaline ratcheted up as far as it can go. The adrenaline bit isn't wrong. But the hype isn't unfounded—I think the difference is self-reliance. Jumpers push themselves in PT every day to be stronger, fitter, and more agile because they're alone out there against the fire. There's no engine coming. No dozer to clear an eight-foot fire line at a particularly vulnerable spot. No helicopter to lift them out of there if the wind shifts. So they tear up the ground with seemingly impossible ferocity because they have to.

Not *they*. *We*.

Every so often, I hear a shout from Griggs, and we all pause, look back, and see a tree lean, then crash to the ground, forcing a cloud of debris into the air and shaking the hillside. I breathe through cramps in my legs and stitches in my side. My shoulders burn with the effort of swinging my Pulaski hard and fast. But a fierce grin fixes itself on my face at the punishing pace we set.

When Aloha and Jason's trenches meet at the top of the ridge, Watters peels off to inspect the far end of the ridge where they had to move too quickly. At the sudden pause in aerobic activity, her whole upper body heaves, drawing breath in and out, trying to coax her lungs into recovery mode.

Aloha turns back to me. "Go swamp for Griggs. Jason and I will finish this line."

I stow my Pulaski and hike back to where Griggs is slicing

through thick sage branches now that the big trees have been toppled. I cinch my gloves and start chucking the slash out of the fire's path, slowing a little as the flames flatten and then go out. When at last the roar of the chainsaw cuts out, I look up to see the crew coming together in the middle of the ridge. The air is thin at the top and clearing quickly as high winds sweep the last of the smoke away. Exhausted, I stumble over to join them. Everybody's swapping high fives and wiping relieved, sooty faces clean.

Griggs smacks the top of my hardhat. "Not bad, rook. *Now* you're a jumper."

Aloha leans back and lets out a whoop that echoes across the valley. Jason claps his arms around me. "We did it," he whispers.

"Yeah, we did." I squeeze back, then let go with a long exhale. I'm not the kind to get weepy easily, except if I'm really, really mad, or when I'm so beat I can't control a single thing I'm doing. Before anybody can see, I swipe a drip of water from the corner of each eye.

I glance up. Watters is watching, leaning on her Pulaski, her face barely recognizable beneath all that ash. She doesn't say anything, doesn't even nod; she only holds my gaze for a moment before blinking slowly in recognition. When her eyes reopen they are looking west, across the rippling Flathead Range, at everything that fire would have eaten up if we weren't there to stop it.

We sit on the ridge, our packs between our knees, while we

dig into our rations. I need to find a tree to hide behind, so I can pee and then jab myself with an insulin shot. We have a full day of work ahead of us, mopping up the burn, stamping out every last bit of that hillside still smoldering. But for now, we take in the view, and the thinning smoke in the air, and all that the eight of us were able to accomplish.

What's absolutely wild—there are homes and towns a couple ridges over. The people living there will probably never know we were here; they'll never know how close that fire came to breaking through.

Part of understanding fire is holding on to a healthy dose of fear. But what nobody tells you is that to fight fire, you have to love it.

Maybe love *isn't the right word—maybe it's more like obsession.*

That's what keeps you going through the tedious days and weeks when all you can do is wait. Well, wait, and break your back working at abatement, two-a-day training sessions, or maintaining and inspecting your gear.

And then things pick up and the waiting is over. If you're lucky, the season doesn't ever tip over from aggressive to alarming. It doesn't ever tumble from invigorating to straight-up terrifying.

CHAPTER 33

AFTER ALL THAT work, sleeping out under the stars, then packing everything back out to the extraction point, and hiding my pricks from the rest of the crew, hell yeah, am I ready for a day off. While Jason makes his calls—first to his little brother, Willie, who passes the phone to their very worried parents, and then a separate call to Janie—I stick myself in the finger and slide the tab into the glucometer, waiting until it and the numbers coming in from my sensor agree that my blood sugar is once again in an acceptable range.

We shower, then pile into Jason's truck, headed for Aunt Cate's. We roll down the windows and turn the music up full blast, which, in his old beater, isn't very loud. Every so often, I find myself howling along, I'm so damn happy. I catch Jason's eye and we both bust up laughing—just because.

We're smokejumpers—have the freaking pin to prove it. We just jumped our first fire, and put it out a whisker before it got away from us. I feel like I could burst—like my cheeks are going to crack if I don't quit smiling soon.

When we pull in, Aunt Cate runs to meet us. "You did it! You really did it!"

"We did." My goofy smile isn't going anywhere anytime soon.

"Nerd."

"Yeah. A big, badass, smokejumping nerd."

Aunt Cate rises onto her tiptoes to squeeze us around the necks. "Well, come on in. We've got some celebrating to do!"

After dinner, Aunt Cate flips through my logs, then goes over the specs for the new pump she's working on for me. Two weeks—I only need to hack my way through for a little longer until the new tech is ready. It's doable, it just isn't going to be easy. Of course, she tries to talk me out of jumping any more until it's ready, but I'm not going to hear it—not from Jason, and not from her.

"Just *tell* them about your condition. By this point, you've clearly demonstrated you can handle the rigors of the job. And you can't be the only wildland firefighter managing diabetes at work—surely there are others."

"I mean, yeah—but it's rare. And how many of them are smokejumpers? I'm betting zero. People already question if I can do this job just because I'm not a guy. No way am I adding a complicated, chronic medical diagnosis to the tally of reasons for them to write me off."

"Look, I know this is your world, Blair. And you know way more about how it works. But I've seen the medical forms—they say diabetes *may* be disqualifying. It's not an absolute. If they want you, and if you show them they can trust you, that with precise monitoring the condition can be safely regulated, then—"

"No."

"Blair"—she slaps her hands against her thighs in exasperation—"you've got to trust people sometime."

"But it's *my* body. Why should anyone else get a say in what I do with it?"

Aunt Cate sighs. "It isn't fair, I know. But for the people who love you—like me, like Jason, like your parents—keeping you alive is the most important thing."

I shake my head. She doesn't understand—without this, I don't have anything. I can't risk this. I just can't.

Later that evening, we sit out by the firepit we dug into the patio a few summers ago. Trapped in their steel barrel, the flames seem so friendly—I have to stop myself from reaching out to touch them. The glow flickers across Jason's face, and Aunt Cate's, and sparks pop and crackle, fizzing into the night air. Everything is as it should be.

But as I stare into the flames, no matter how many times I snatch it back, my mind keeps drifting to Watters. Is she still pissed? Does she still think of me as a kid? Is she thinking of me at all? I realize too late that I missed something either Jason or Aunt Cate said. Both are staring, their heads cocked, waiting for me to notice the long, drawn-out silence.

Jason shakes his head, clucking his tongue. "Blair's got it bad."

"Do not," I fire back. How does he know?

"Well, this I need to hear." Aunt Cate arches an eyebrow.

"No, you don't," I mutter.

"She was one of our instructors." Jason flinches away from my swipe.

"So she's old?"

"She isn't *old*. She's, like, twenty-four or something."

Aunt Cate bites her lip, blinking at my rush to defend the woman I'm allegedly not at all interested in. Shit. There'll be no stuffing that back in the bag.

"Ha haaaa—see? It's so obvious anytime Watters and Blair are near each other—anybody in a ten-mile radius could pick it up."

"They cannot."

"You should see them when they go out for a run together. It's, like—orgasmic or something."

"Jason Wallace, if you don't shut the hell up, I swear to god—"

He shrinks back, cackling.

"It's nothing. She barely knows I exist."

"Oh, Blair." Aunt Cate tilts her head on an angle, sending me a pitying look.

"Don't believe her." Jason dips his head back, eyes on the sky. "Blair's so busy making sure nobody can find even one chink in that armor of hers, she never lets anybody in."

Aunt Cate clucks her tongue. "Now, that's a shame."

"Yep."

"*Come on*, you guys." I'm dying here.

Aunt Cate's head rests against the tall back of her Adirondack chair. She looks into the fire, purposefully away from me. "It's not the worst thing in the world to find someone worth showing your soft underbelly to."

"Please stop. I am literally begging you both."

Aunt Cate reaches across the space between us and clasps my hand. "If you're invincible, then you're not human." She squeezes, hard. "It's okay to be vulnerable. Sometimes that's the bravest thing a person can do."

We pull into the parking lot on base later that night, laughing, music blaring, only to find a very different atmosphere than we left. People are running between the loft and the offices, expressions grim. When we park in front of the dorm, Dirk hustles out to meet us.

"Where have you guys been?"

Jason and I trade confused looks.

"We had the day off."

"You don't take your phones with you?"

Realization dawns on Jason's face. I unsling my CamelBak and unzip the front pocket. "There's no reception at my aunt's house."

I unlock the home screen to find more than twenty messages waiting.

"We must not have heard the messages dinging in on the way home . . ."

". . . because the music was up full blast."

"Oops."

A frown creases Dirk's face. "Follow me."

We set off at a brisk walk toward Operations. It seems like everybody on base is packed in there, with a phone or radio pressed to their ear or studying the map stretched across the table. I scoot against the wall, out of everybody's way, while Dirk quickly fills us in.

"Jumpers from the McCall base were called out on a series of lightning strikes yesterday. They were able to suppress three of them, but a fourth was deemed to be in a let-burn area of the forest that needed clearing out."

"Let me guess—conditions changed and now it's headed toward some structures?"

"Yeah. Eighty-mile-an-hour winds blew it way off course, where a handcrew in its path sustained some serious burns. They're down manpower, and since resources are already deployed all over the West, there's not much more to give.

"The fire is now headed straight toward Sun Valley. The National Guard is on its way. Station crews are evacuating the whole town, and fully half the resources fighting the Tahoe fire have been redirected to mitigate structure damage up in Idaho, including a whole crew from our base. That leaves us with barely one crew left here, counting you two."

Dirk swallows, and his eyes go a little wide. "And the three of us rookies are half of what's left. Hawkins is pissed."

Rookies. Still?

"If we weren't here, they'd already be out of jumpers," I say.

"True. But we still make them nervous."

"What more could we possibly do to prove ourselves? We've done *everything* they've asked!"

"Blair," Jason whispers. "Keep it down."

Dirk motions toward the door and we make our way back outside. "For now, get yourselves ready. Get your gear prepped and your head right. If we're lucky, a call won't come in before some more of our crew gets back here."

He frowns. "But I wouldn't count on it."

Fire Watch-Out Situations

No. 9: Building fireline downhill with fire below.

CHAPTER 34

THE CALL COMES too soon, when the jump list is still piti-
fully short. Admin even brings old Frank back from retirement to
be the spotter so Aloha can jump with us. Three sticks load into
the aircraft: Aloha and me, Dirk and Watters, Griggs and Jason.
While the engine roars to life, Aloha shouts, "It's as good a spot as
we could hope for. I've hiked that section of the forest before. We'll
zip this up in half a day and hustle back to the base, ready for the
next call that comes in, no problem."

Dirk watches out the window while Aloha speaks, not looking
reassured one bit. When the plane circles over the fire, I finally
feel that knot of tension release—there's a wide-open meadow to
land in, with a river cutting through the landscape that no fire
will be jumping. Maybe Aloha's right—this will be a straightfor-
ward day.

Frank picks the north end of the meadow as our jump spot—
far away from the moving water. We watch the streamers hit the

ground while the plane banks. Below, the river slithers by, the meadow grasses roiling in a slurry of contrary gusts.

Time to go. My adrenaline spikes as the shouted instructions begin, stick after stick.

I clip in. Wait. My guts drop down to my toes.

Slap.

I launch into the air, the wind roaring at me while I tuck, counting. When my chute snicks open, my legs swing up to touch the horizon. I don't take my usual time enjoying the scenery—even though the river is far enough away, I do *not* want to land anywhere near the water. Instead, I study the fire below.

West of the river and the meadow, a series of rolling hills wrinkle the landscape. The fire gnaws at the scrub, eating up the ground as the wind pushes it toward the town of Elk River. The fire is small still, just as Aloha said, the smoke rolling in a slow-moving plume. With the reservoir to the south and a web of rivers snaking through the valleys, this one shouldn't have anywhere to run.

I turn my attention to the jump spot in the meadow below. After landing on slopes and rocky hillsides, dodging snags and stumps, touching down at the end of a wide meadow sounds like pure heaven. Still, the ground comes up quick, as it always does—I make a last-minute adjustment, clap my feet together, then land and roll in one fluid movement. Other than one flailing arm on landing, it was a textbook PLF; I hop up, stow my gear, and head straight to engage the fire.

One by one, we fall in. Smoke curls around our legs, the glaring sun over my shoulder shooting beams of ashy light through the cracks in the thickening plume of smoke. A headache starts, dull but insistent. Hours roll by and we work steady and hard. I'm draining my canteens too fast, but I can't seem to quench my thirst. I gnaw on some gummies. My hair is slick, my ribs dripping with sweat. The longer we work, the hotter that chemical fire inside of me burns.

Fire in my arms and legs. Fire in my lungs. Fire searing the length of me.

Adrenaline. Cortisol. Dopamine. Insulin.

Or the lack of it.

"Blair!" The voice sounds far away.

Is that Jason? Why is he shouting?

Why is everything so blurry?

Why am I sitting down?

"I'm fine," I call out, not sure which direction he's coming from. "I just need a minute."

His boots come into view—I blink, but can't get my eyes to clear. He squats low, peering into my face. "You don't look fine."

I squeeze my eyes shut. "I'm wearing my sensor—my watch hasn't pulsed in hours. I should be fine."

"Hours? You haven't gotten a reading in *hours*?"

I shut my eyes, trying to remember. "Not since we were in the ready room."

"That's not normal." He sounds scared. "Not without an insulin pump automatically regulating your levels."

"But—why?" I can't focus. I can't *think*.

"Let me see that." Jason draws my wrist up and taps through the apps on my watch. "It's blank. Blair, your transmitter isn't sending anything."

I peel down my waistband. The sensor is right there, with the transmitter intact. It's just no longer stuck to my skin.

"Oh. I guess it's hot today," I mumble.

"Too much sweat? The tape came off?"

When I don't answer, Jason does the thinking for me. "You took your long-acting shot this morning?"

"Yeah."

"And I saw you give yourself that rapid-acting shot at lunch. So you have a baseline level of insulin in your system. But something went wrong anyway." He fishes a packet of gummies out of his pants pocket and feeds them to me, one at a time, like I'm a baby bird or something. But my head is all wiggly on top of my neck, so maybe I need it.

"Come on, let's get you back to the safe zone."

"No, I can do this." To prove it, I heft myself up to standing.

But once I get there, I pitch and sway, and would have slid right back to the ground if Jason didn't prop me upright.

"Blair, come on. You're clearly—"

"All that's left," I interrupt. "You heard them. We're it. We have to contain this fire."

Jason grimaces. He scans the area, and the others clearing brush and cutting line. "You are not swinging a Pulaski in this condition."

"No—Aloha will demand a reason, and then they'll all know, and that will be the end for me. I can't—"

"I'm not covering for you this time, Blair."

"Jason!"

"I won't. You *know* the risks. Blindness. Brain damage. Death. It's too dangerous. I'm not covering for you anymore, not if you refuse to take care of yourself." Jason lifts his radio to his mouth. "Aloha, this is Jason."

"Go."

"Blair is joining Dirk at his lookout post."

The receiver crackles with Aloha's response.

"I'm taking her there, then I'll explain when I meet up on the other side with you all," Jason says.

He turns his grimace on me. I'm furious—or I would be if I could think clearly enough. But every bit of that fury is met by an equal amount of fear written all over his face.

"When we get back to base, you have exactly two minutes to report your condition to Hawkins or I'm doing it for you."

"Okay."

Jason lets out a long sigh and glances at the fire rolling up the hills at the southwest end of the meadow. "Let's cut across the black below the burn. It'll be shorter."

I grunt. "I can go around like everybody else."

"We are not taxing your systems by hiking one step farther than we have to. Look—Watters and Griggs are already buttoning up the heel. We cut across the black to the west flank and up to that outcropping where Dirk is posted. We won't get anywhere near the active fire, and you can park it on lookout duty until this fire is contained."

If I weren't spooked myself, I'd argue. But I'm still fighting for every breath. I still can't quite see straight.

We march diagonally across the meadow. The soil beneath our feet is charred and uneven, still smoldering. I step carefully, and I don't shake off Jason's steadying grip on my elbow. Off my left shoulder, the fire creeps upward, nearly cresting a low hill to the west.

A rumble sounds, careening through the valley. I twist around, trying to pinpoint where, exactly, the sound is coming from. I cock my head, listening. Is that a tanker coming in from the reservoir? I didn't hear any chatter about air support.

The radio beeps and squawks. It's Dirk. "Terrain unsteady. Repeat—I'm seeing movement on the hillside—"

But the rest of his warning is lost as the rumble becomes a roar. I glance up in time to see a half dozen boulders hurtling down the hill. I don't even have time to draw breath before they tumble all around me, one whisking so close it knocks my hardhat askew. I suck in a breath, spin around, and yell for everybody to get out of the way.

But no one is looking at me.

They are all staring at the ground behind me. And then they start running.

My mind unspools, rewinding to separate the sound of rock striking the dirt and that other sound—that meaty *thwack* of hard meeting soft, of expelled breath and crushed bones. I whirl around. Jason is on the ground, arched awkwardly like a beetle on its back. There is a peculiar dent in his chest below the collar of his dirty yellow shirt; a rock the size of a mailbox lies inert a few feet away. I stare, uncomprehending, while Dirk and Griggs skid to a stop beside Jason's limp body.

Radio chatter bats at my head. Hands grip me, shaking.

No. He's fine.

The whole crew is on the ground at my feet, taking Jason's pulse and, when that doesn't work, feeling for any sign of breath.

He's fine—just give him some space.

Panic throttles my airway. I can't breathe. I can't think. If everyone would just quit shouting—

He's fine. He'll be fine in a minute.

Aloha is speaking into the radio, calm and clear. *Crushed chest cavity. Extraction point.* I try to swim through his words—it's like when you've been tossed by a wave to the seafloor and you can't tell which way is up, the sand swirling all around you, the froth making it impossible to see; your breath is running out and if your feet can't find the ground to launch your body back up, you never will break the surface.

Recover the body tomorrow.

That does it—air flows down my throat and into my lungs.

Jason.

I drop to my knees, scrabbling at the others to get out of the way. I cup his face in my hands. His eyes are open, staring at nothing. His hands, for once, are still, fingers curled up.

"Jason?"

Somebody's trying to pull me away.

"He just needs a minute. Jason!"

High above, the clouds groan and churn. One shelf of air rises to the heavens while another thrusts suddenly downward. With a whine, the winds at ground level tumble over themselves, changing course like a herd of startled buffalo. The flames shriek in response, veering east where tasseled grasses haven't yet burned.

"Um," Dirk says as columns of smoke whip past our faces, pricking at our eyes and shoving up our nostrils. "That wind just reversed. It's going to blow the fire right back over our position."

"We need to move, and now," Aloha orders.

Hands grab my shoulders, tugging. I shake them off. My head is beginning to clear—enough to know for certain that Jason can't hike. And if he can't leave, then no way am I going anywhere. He isn't alone in this—he can't be. We've always taken our hits together—borne any pain across both our shoulders. That's just how it is.

Watters kneels down to look me in the eyes. "We'll come back for the body."

The body?

"Blair, we have to go."

"I'm not leaving him," I whisper.

Dirk crouches on my other side. "Blair, come on. That fire is coming straight toward us. There's nothing more we can do for him right now."

"I'm not leaving!"

Aloha grabs my arm but I whip it away with a growl.

"You're going to die out here, and for no reason. I'm the JIC and I'm ordering you to hike out now."

They grab me, try to pull me with them, but I'm like a wild thing, flailing, lashing out. I am *not* leaving him here. I break free, swaying to my feet, glancing around, frantic. Those flames cannot have him. I won't allow it. I struggle across the meadow to wrench a downed branch free. I hack at the spurs until the branch is smooth enough, then roll it under Jason's left side. Wedging my Pulaski under the right, I cinch my letdown rope across Jason's crushed chest, securing his body onto the makeshift travois. All the while, he just lies there, lifeless, as the fire creeps closer.

"Blair, *come on*," Yolo pleads.

The flames crackle and pop, smoke ripping past us.

"Blair!" Aloha yells. "We can't bring both of you—that fire is moving too fast. And we can't leave you here."

They come for me one last time, but I stumble away. They're confused, hurt, panicked.

"Blair!"

Shut up. Everybody just shut up.

"Don't be a fool."

"Just go."

I bend my knees like I'm getting ready for a deadlift. I grip the loop I tied at the end of the rope and pull, wincing at the cruel weight. Fire has nearly closed off the exit route. With a last frustrated look back, the rest of my crew heads for the extraction point at a fast clip, leaving me behind.

I suck in a wavering breath. All I have to do is make it to the river and that stretch of sand beyond the high-water line. I take off at a run, or the closest thing to one I can manage, my boots scrabbling to bite deep into the soil for purchase. I don't look back over my shoulder, though I feel the fire behind me, hear it crackling, nipping at my heels.

Grass fires are lightning fast—I almost make it to the silty beach when the flames catch me, leaping forward, licking at the poles and Jason's boots, and reaching for the back of my hardhat. The smell of singeing hair and burning rubber is sharp in my nostrils. I drop the travois, cut the branch loose, and hurl it away from us. I yank my fire shelter off my pack as the hiss of flames scrapes at my ears. I stand at Jason's feet, shake the shelter open, then step on the far loop and drop to the ground on top of him, cinching the other loop over our heads. I lie there, covering his body and my own with the fire shelter while the flames roar over us, sudden gusts prying at my grip and trying to rip the fabric out of my hands. I tuck my face in the gap between Jason's shoulders and where his head rests on the ground, sucking in ragged breaths.

The fire rages, the air inside the shelter growing hotter and hotter, smoke seeping in at the edges. *I'm going to die right here.* The thought alone should send me into hysterics—I should scream at the bad luck that took Jason from me. I should be sobbing at the thought of never hiking with Aunt Cate again, or never laughing at something ridiculous Yolo or one of the guys said—the feeling of a hot shower after a brutal week cutting line, or losing myself in the middle of the wilderness.

But it doesn't send me over the edge. If anything, the gusting flames calm me, cut through the fog like nothing else has. I hold on to the handles even as the heat becomes unbearable, as the wind tears at the edges, trying to wrest loose the thin shield that is the only barrier between our bodies and those flames. My knuckles singe and my lungs burn.

If he didn't make it through this, neither should I.

The fire keens and moans, a dirge of ghostly voices, beckoning.

« « NOW « «

Maintain control of your forces at all times.

STANDARD FIREFIGHTING ORDERS, NO. 9

CHAPTER 35

"EXCEPT YOU DIDN'T die."

Officer Molt frowns at the blinking red light on the recorder. He flips back through his notes, chewing on the edge of his mustache. "You refused orders to evacuate with the rest of the crew, and in so doing, you exposed yourself and your crew to unnecessary risk. This action also required you to be picked up at a later time, it is worth noting, at considerable cost to taxpayers."

Taxpayers. Seriously? "I wasn't going to leave Jason behind."

Officer Molt sighs. "Noble. But stupid."

I'm not doing this anymore. He's gone. What does any of it even matter? "Are we done here?"

"Almost." He flips through the stack of papers. "You radioed for an exit at oh-seven-hundred this morning. The report states that the rescue boat found you on the bank of the Little North Fork Clearwater River in a burned-out section of the forest. Jason Wallace's body had been cut free of a travois held together with

sliced sections of letdown rope. Another infraction that will probably come out of your paycheck."

"Is there a question in there somewhere?"

"The report also states that there were signs of a struggle of
some sort in the sand around the body. Coyotes, maybe?"

Bastard. "And this is part of your official investigation?"

"I'm only trying to get to the bottom of—"

"Fuck you."

Molt clears his throat, twice, then shuffles the papers together
and closes the file. He leans over, speaking into the recorder. "This
concludes my interview with Blair E. Scott . . ."

I don't wait for him to finish. I scrape back my chair and bang
out the door. I lift a hand to the wall when I reach the hallway—
I'm going to pass out if I don't eat something. I'm supposed to
report to the doctor as well, to get the burns on my hands checked
out. But if I don't get out of these filthy clothes, I'm going to lose
what little might be left of my sanity.

I make for the dorm, head down, avoiding eye contact—not
that anybody is ready to talk to me. I don't bother stopping at my
room for towels or shampoo or anything. I get to the bathroom,
where a charred, wild animal stares back at me in the mirror.
There's no flush of life to my skin, nothing but the pale wash of
shock. I begin peeling off my clothes. I pull off my socks and chuck
my phone on top of the pile. I'm going to have to call Jason's mom

and tell her. And Janie. A sob slides free and I give up fiddling with the buttons at my waist.

I sweep back the vinyl curtain to the nearest shower and turn the faucet on, full blast, no matter that I'm still in my pants and sports bra. I don't have the energy to fight anymore. I pump the soap dispenser bolted to the wall and scrub my arms, my face, my hair. Black soap bubbles swirl down the drain while I scrub and scrub, the burns on my hands screaming in protest, until at last the water runs clean.

At some point, I figure out how to slide out of the crusty green pants, but it's too much effort to step out of them, so they circle my ankles like Nomex shackles. The water goes from scalding hot to lukewarm to bitterly cold, and I shrink away, sliding to the tile floor as it pummels me from above.

Whatever Molt decides, I'll never forgive myself. I don't want to. Jason was only crossing that meadow in that spot because of me.

I was *right there*. It's all my fault.

My teeth chatter, my whole body convulses. I'm so cold—I should have taken off all my clothes—the wet fabric only makes the chill sink into my bones. I can hardly open my fingers to reach for the levers to turn off the shower.

The line between life and death is sometimes wide as a fire break cut by the sharpened blade of a bulldozer. Other times, it's thin as the whisper of breath that coaxes flame from coals. Every day on the job, wildland firefighters walk that line, one foot in the black, one foot in the green—one foot in life, one foot in death.

All it takes is one step in either direction. One step.

Right now, a single step is too much to ask.

"One foot in the black," I whisper, like saying it out loud will make me believe I could actually drag myself out of this. "One foot in the green, one foot in the black."

I lose track of how many times I say it.

Jason would hate this. I want out of here. I want to warm up. I want to feel the sun on my skin. But I can't seem to move. The last thing I remember is the sound of my head hitting the tile, my hair landing in the pooling water like a wet mop slapping the floor.

Fire Watch-Out Situations

No. 8: Constructing line without safe anchor point.

CHAPTER 36

"BLAIR!"

The voice sounds like it's coming from the other end of a long tunnel. Something smacks against my cheek.

"Blair!" The voice is closer now.

It's Watters. *What?* "Why are you all wet?"

She doesn't answer—her head slumps onto her hand and she rakes her fingers through her hair.

"Because I had to drag your ass out of that freezing shower." There's a hiccup in her voice. "Jesus, Blair. You scared the shit out of me."

"The shower? But I'm so cold."

"Yeah. If you're going to off yourself, hypothermia is about the worst way to do it."

"I would never—Jason would kill me."

Jason. That knife sinks straight into my chest, and twists. My head drops back—it's so heavy. And then a horrible screaming sound starts up—some animal behind the dorm must be making one hell of a racket.

"Shhhhh. Shhhhh." Watters wraps her arms around my shoulders.

I close my mouth. The awful noise stops.

"Come on. We've got to warm you up." Watters hooks her arms under my armpits, stands, and drags me out of the bathroom and down the hall to my room.

I squeeze my eyes shut. I can't bear to see it—my messy pile of laundry, the harmonica teetering on the windowsill—everything as it was before my whole world ended. Before Jason—

I crash onto the bed, then Watters yanks off my pants and my underwear. She tugs at my bra for a few seconds before giving up—the fabric may as well be suction-cupped to my skin. The rasp of scissors scrapes the air and it's off. Watters tears through my closet, pulls out my sleeping bag, stuffs my limbs inside, and zips the thing all the way up to my chin.

She taps her phone with one hand, taking my pulse with the other. "Nineteen, female. Hypothermia. Yes. Yes. No—wait, maybe diabetes. She's got a device of some kind and the skin on her abdomen is covered in needle marks."

Oh.

Shit.

Watters sets the phone on speaker to answer another flurry of questions confirming the address and my vitals while she chafes her hands along the length of my legs.

There's a pause, and then she leans in to whisper, "You're going to be okay. I've got you."

When my eyelids begin to feel heavy, Watters slaps my cheeks again, glaring, inches away from my face. "No. You are not going to sleep right now, Blair. No way."

Instead, I focus on her eyes, dark as a thunderstorm, and pleading.

My voice slurs, "You're so pretty."

That makes her even angrier. "Save it."

The door bangs open and a team of paramedics rushes in. There's beeping, and people shouting all these questions. So many questions. Watters backs against the wall as they strap me onto the gurney and wheel me outside.

After the flames have died down, smothered under a blanket of slurry or drowned in buckets of water dropped from a helicopter or burning itself up when the fuel is gone, fire still lives under the surface. It smolders beneath blackened dirt, gnawing out the core of twisting tree roots. Even when the ground is no longer smoking, when the mud churned up by heat and water has ceased boiling, fire lives beneath the surface, waiting for the chance to flare back to life.

CHAPTER 37

WHEN I WAKE next, the sun swipes across my face, scraping my dry and bloodshot eyes. I take a deep breath, stretching my arms over my head and yawning, my back arching like a cat. There's the familiar smell of cedar-lined closets, and vetiver soap—we must be at Aunt Cate's. I relax against the pillow, tucking my grandma's quilt under my arms.

And then I remember—not we. Not anymore.

I roll onto my side, punching my pillow over my head to shut out the sound of birds chirping in the tree outside the window, to shut out the world spinning when it should have stopped dead in its orbit. Bandages over my knuckles seep red. Stars burst against my eyelids, lancing inward.

I want it all gone. All of it. I shove it all away.

I open my eyes. It's morning. I go out to the hall bathroom, past my phone making a pathetic beeping sound while the battery dies. I chuck it down the stairs, pee, then stumble back to bed.

It's the middle of the night. I stare through the window slats at a half-moon. It's neon pink from all the smoke in the air. My eyes flutter closed, my eyelids rough as sandpaper.

The moon is gone. Sunlight streams through the window. Aunt Cate is standing over me with a bowl of something in her hand, yelling at me to eat. I groan and turn over. My eyelids drift closed again.

Ever since my first summer as a volunteer with the county, since my first day on camp crew, since the first time I saw a load of jumpers drop out of the sky, fire burned me up from the inside. Chemical fire whispering in my ear, licking the length of my bones, tasting the surface of my skin, and filling every inch of me with light, with life itself. But now fire hurts. It burns too hot, makes me feel too much. It's going to eat me alive.

Fire is not my friend. Not anymore.

That flame inside me is snuffed out. My limbs grow stiff, my insides run instead with ice water, layer after layer of water dousing the space where my lungs used to flare and seize with so much power, where my heart used to beat.

Cold takes me, suspends my broken heart in a block of ice, so I never have to open myself to that fire again.

· · ·

Hours later.

Or maybe it's days. I don't know—even sleep has left me. The door squeaks open. Aunt Cate ducks her head inside.

"I cleaned out his dorm at the base and moved his things into yours. Is there anything you want here, now?"

I can hear the words, but they don't make any sense. I want Jason back. What else could possibly matter?

Aunt Cate lays out some clothes. I register the words *funeral* and *flight home*, something about escorting a casket. Everything goes dark, but only for a second. If only I *could* black out.

Then, softly, "We have to go, Blair."

Identify escape routes and safety zones
and make them known.

Standard Firefighting Orders, No. 4

CHAPTER 38

THEY HOLD THE funeral at some church back home in Gunbarrel. Nineteen-year-olds don't make wills, so Jason's parents made all the decisions.

They greet me on the way in. His dad pulls me into a bear hug, sobbing. I sort of pat his back, thinking how much his bulk draped over me feels different from Jason, even though they have the same big frame. Jason's mom is staring fixedly away; she won't even look at me.

That's okay. I blame me, too.

Then Janie is in front of me. She's tiny—if I look straight ahead, I don't have to see her eyes, red and puffy. She's pleading, but my ears may as well be stuffed with cotton—I can't hear the words. I don't want to hear everything I should have done differently.

Just in time, the music picks up. Everybody shuffles to find a seat, while a couple of Jason's linebacker buddies wave me over. I follow them back outside, relieved to be out of that place. It reeks of grief.

But my relief only lasts for a second—the church lawn is filled with people from high school: a random clump of people to the left, and the entire football squad on the right, wearing their jerseys. Everybody's watching two big screens where pictures of Jason wink in and out.

I fix my gaze on my feet.

I was the one putting myself in danger, over and over again.

I was the one being reckless. I was the one who was supposed to die.

The guys stop walking when they reach the parking lot. Jason's little brother, Willie, can barely fill out the shoulders of his rented tux. The sleeves, reaching down to his knuckles, quiver.

I should put my arm around him. Or something.

But I don't.

I blink, confused. It's good to be outside, away from all those people, but why—

A shiny black car with a super-long hatchback pulls up to the curb. Oh.

Some guy in a suit that's clearly seen some wear gets out of the driver's seat and arranges our little huddle into two lines. I look to the guy beside me, suddenly disoriented. I'm never disoriented. I always know where I am—I've always got the landmarks memorized and the topography burned into my brain. So why isn't Yolo in Missoula? What is he doing in Gunbarrel, in line with those dummies in football jerseys?

A blunt weight is lowered onto my shoulder. I shift so the wood isn't so much resting on my shoulder as propped in my arms, like it's some new CrossFit challenge and not Jason up there, lifeless, in a wooden box.

Willie is sniffling now, hanging on to the coffin more than holding it up. Why couldn't I just give the kid a hug?

Then we're striding down the sidewalk between the two masses of high school kids, inside the church's double doors, and down that long aisle. I can't think about what it is I'm actually doing, so I focus on my arms, the burn in my biceps—that feels good. The fire in my triceps—nice.

Then we're at the pulpit, where two massive portraits flank a low table covered in flowers. I don't know who's steering things, but we end up filing to either side of the platform and lowering the coffin on top. There must have been some meeting I didn't get the notice about because after that, everybody scatters. I hover there for a second, that cavernous room full of people leering at me.

There's no map for this, no topo line to trace—no escape route to be found. I'm like a compass needle that can't feel the earth—spinning and spinning with nowhere to land.

Somebody stands in the pews to the right—it's Aunt Cate. She beckons, indicating the empty spot beside her. I stumble down the steps and away from all those eyes as fast as I can. Some guy in churchy robes starts talking, smiling and making jokes like this is a potluck he's hosting or something. And the way he's talking about Jason, like he was the favorite altar boy or something— none of it makes sense. Jason wasn't religious. Why would they bother pretending he was? I glance down the row at Jason's parents, and Willie, who's got his head in his hands now, sobbing. This whole show may be about Jason, but it isn't *for* him. It's for them.

People are shuffling programs, but I don't have anything to do with my hands. They keep taking turns at the podium. Some try to tell funny stories. Everybody is crying. Then Janie gets up there and reads the lyrics to that Billy Joel song Jason was always singing her.

I watch it all through a fog, confused more than anything. He was here, three days ago. Alive. Bursting with life.

Nothing makes sense.

Then his football buddies get up there and they're trying to be all tough or something. They make some comment about Billy Joel, and what a good guy Jason was, and how he was too young, and—

No. Whose idea was this? "Only the Good Die Young" prances out from the speakers, cheerful and irreverent. People stand up and clap along like it's a gospel song or something.

I can't sit through this. Fuck.

"Don't—" Aunt Cate grabs my arm.

I shake her off and make for the fizzling EXIT sign at a run.

Fire Watch-Out Situations

No. 7: No communication link with crew members or supervisor.

CHAPTER 39

I AM ICE. I am bitter cold. Not even a whisper of flame.

Hours crawl past.

Days roll into weeks.

Summer bends its knee, giving way to fall.

But out there, an impossible distance away, out in the wilderness, the fires burn on.

Aunt Cate stands over me, yelling until I sit up, then huffing a sigh of relief, then yelling some more until I stand and let her click in my new insulin pump and sensor. More yelling until I pee, brush my teeth, and get my ass in the Jeep. Only once I'm loaded in, seat belt fastened, does the yelling stop. Aunt Cate gets in, starts up the engine, and drives. It's no better being awake in a moving vehicle than in my bed. I slump against the window frame, begging for sleep.

. . .

Hours later, Aunt Cate pulls up to an empty trailhead and hops out. I climb reluctantly out of the Jeep. I have to pee again.

When I clamber out of the brush, Aunt Cate is strapping a pack onto her back that reaches at least a foot over her head.

"What are you doing?" I ask. "Two steps and you're going to topple over backward."

"So you smokejumpers really are just overstuffed egos like everybody says?"

I glare at her. So hard.

"You're not the only one who can hike with a heavy pack."

I fling my arms out to the side. "What are we doing out here?"

"Camping."

"Camping. Now?"

"Right now." Aunt Cate clips her keys into a zippered pocket on her hip belt and starts up the trail.

"But I didn't pack anything. No tent, no sleeping bag, no water filter. I can't go camping."

"I've got it all."

"I'm in flip-flops!"

Aunt Cate twists back around. "You're going to want those for camp tonight; clip them on to your hip. Your boots and a pair of socks are behind your seat."

She starts up the trail again. I glower after her, seriously considering getting back in the Jeep, curling up in the back seat, and waiting her out. But I don't have a cell phone—I couldn't call anyone to come get me even if there was a single person at this point who'd pick up. I don't even have a granola bar or a water bottle.

"Shit." I wrench open the door and sit, reaching around to fish my socks and shoes out of the back. Once they're on, I slam the door and follow the trail over the low rise.

Aunt Cate's a fast hiker. Not that I should be surprised—she's the one who taught me how to hike, and how to survive in the wilderness. How to fish. How to start a fire without a match. How to hunt for our dinner. How to sit in the silence of untouched wilderness and let it wash over me, scrubbing all the chaos of civilized life out of my bones. How to remind myself that I'm just another wild animal with a big brain and some handy tools.

After the first mile, I've stopped being pissed that Aunt Cate dragged me out there. Without a pack on, the trail is easy, no matter how steeply my fitness has dropped off. By the second mile, the creaky feeling has worn off and my eyes are drawn up to the sunlight streaking through the trees and the critters hiding in the branches above.

I cough a lot, though, my lungs clearing themselves of cold, stale air. By the third mile, I'm breathing hard, though a trail like this should be nothing more than a warm-up, even considering my current piss-poor fitness level. It doesn't make any sense—I'm not packing a single ounce. I'm like a child, not even carrying my own water weight.

But the miles begin to clear my head along with my lungs, and soon, ragged steps crack and thaw all that's frozen inside me, breaking through to the soft, tender places beneath. As the ice recedes, I'm forced to *feel*—the heaviness weighing on me, pulling me down.

Guilt. Crushing, inescapable guilt. I'll never get away from it.

I pause at a switchback and face the empty expanse. With a whimper, I shut my eyes and let go.

Nothing happens.

And everything.

Pain scrabbles up my legs. A roaring sound smacks at my head. Streaks of red slash across my vision. All that *feeling* swarms and I double over, hacking, spitting, desperate to let it out.

Then, as suddenly as it began, it's over. I blink, turn uphill, and keep plodding. The numb is gone. Loss pries at the muscles spanning my back. Guilt settles low and hard in my belly. Grief crushes my sternum. But I can breathe around it, and through it.

There's nothing else to do—nothing else I *can* do.

I keep walking.

We camp that night beside an alpine lake. Aunt Cate turns her back while she lights the stove and stirs her dehydrated blend of elk strips, veggies, and spices into something that smells so good it has no business coming out of a Ziploc bag.

I take my first bites slowly, exhaling around my spork to let out the steam. I practically inhale the rest, while Aunt Cate pretends not to track each bite going into my mouth. She fills the mug with a second helping, and for the first time in weeks, the creases across her forehead smooth a little.

Nobody suggests a campfire.

We stretch out on our sleeping pads, heads poking out of our bivvies so we can watch the stars spin above. I lie on my back, probing the ache beneath my sternum. It hurts, so much. But somehow it *is* Jason, or at least, what I have left of him. So I rest my hands over my breastbone, like I'm greeting an old friend, and drift off to sleep that way.

After a fire has come and gone, the land waits, scarred and smoking. Days grow short; the north wind sighs from Canada clear down the ripple of the Rocky Mountains, burying the charred earth in mounds and drifts of snow.

Spent, scorned, the land rests.

When the days stretch longer once more, snowmelt sinks into the blackened soil, wetting the husks of seeds cracked open by the fire's heat. Green shoots poke through the soil: hollyhock, fireweed, pine grass. A riot of new growth; a fresh start. But for years, passersby will dismiss the forest as scarred—ugly, even.

Unless you look closely, you'll only see death. You won't see how green things have taken root, winding through every stretch of soil, all through the burn. And then, one day, a riot of life is all you'll see.

Life is stubborn once it's taken hold.

CHAPTER 40

WE STAY OUT in the woods for a week. Aunt Cate is nothing short of a magician, packing all that food into a single backpack— but we have plenty of water, moving between alpine lakes. By the time we pack out, my muscles have begun to remember them- selves again. Aunt Cate still won't let me carry a thing, no matter how much I protest.

The whole drive home, my legs twitch, restless. They're done with walking—I want to run, long and hard. When we pull into the drive, Aunt Cate waves off my efforts to help unpack and hang everything out to dry, so I go inside, shovel down some food, shower, suit up, and take off at a run.

Of course, when I get back home, it's right back to the shower again. I've just lowered myself onto the bed, groaning at the sweet luxury of a pillow beneath my head, when a knock sounds on Aunt Cate's front door.

I roll over to face the wall; whoever it is knocks again. I jam a pillow over my head to block out the sound. Aunt Cate's footsteps sound on the stairs, followed by a low conversation outside my door. Then a knock.

"You have some visitors."

"I don't want to see anyone."

"Tough." The door swings open. It's Watters.

I shoot up, backing against the headboard.

"Be nice." Aunt Cate gives me one of her looks before heading back downstairs again.

Watters gestures for the others to wait, little more than bulky shadows that, after weeks together, I'd probably recognize even in pitch dark. Watters shuts the door behind her, drags a chair over beside the bed, and leans in, elbows on her knees and her face in my face where I can't ignore her.

I cross my arms over my chest.

Watters sighs. "The investigation is finally over. You've been cleared to return to active jumper status—with a doctor's approval and continuous monitoring, obviously. Believe me, Hawkins isn't happy that you didn't disclose your diabetes diagnosis and seek treatment when your tech failed. And I get it—*I'm* pissed at you. But it isn't uncommon for candidates to hide injuries or other complications to avoid washing out. You'd be surprised at the number of guys who've come forward to defend what you did—in that regard, at least."

She pauses, waiting for me to meet her eyes. I don't.

"It matters that you saw a doctor before your first jump onto a fire where your condition could have compromised the rest of the crew. You weren't grounded, so technically you didn't violate the rules." She sits back, and sighs. "There is nothing *normal* about this fire season. We all have extra stresses dictating the decisions we make, every one of us."

I stare at the slats of light glaring through the window until my eyes start to sting and well up. "It doesn't matter what the investigation concluded. I'm not jumping again, not ever." I hadn't said it aloud before, and those words coming out of my own mouth feel like fire searing every inch of me.

"Well, that would be a damn shame."

I swipe at my cheek and the traitor tears there.

"What if I said we need you out there? What if I said *you* need to be out there? What if I said Jason would want—"

"Don't." I meet her eyes, so she knows I mean it.

Watters shakes her head, crisp even in her dissatisfaction.

On its own, my hand reaches for hers, but she shakes that away, too.

"Listen, I know grief. I've been there. I may not be your instructor anymore, but I'm not going to be your distraction either." She searches my face, the divot between her eyebrows pinching, then releasing when she finds what she was looking for.

"You've been going at this like a lone wolf. Jason had your trust, but apparently none of the rest of us did. Out there, we work as a team."

She stands and opens the door, waving Yolo and Griggs inside. "None of us would make it on our own out there, Blair. You're only alone if you choose to be."

Fire Watch-Out Situations

No. 11: Unburned fuel between you and fire.

CHAPTER 41

I GO BACK to the endocrinologist, who lays into me for not disclosing that I was a smokejumper during my first visit. But after scouring my readouts and the monitoring plan Hawkins laid out, she grudgingly signs a medical release. Later that day, I deliver the form to Operations.

Hawkins frowns over the paper. "You know I'll be calling the office to confirm?"

I nod.

"You can stop beating yourself up. We wouldn't ask you back if we didn't want you."

Bullshit. "Yeah, okay."

He sighs, running a hand through what's left of his hair. "I'm not going to say you were right to hide your condition. But if you'd disclosed the diabetes when you arrived for training, we would've sent you right back home. I'm guessing you figured as much, which is why you did what you did."

I nod.

Hawkins shrugs, waiting until I meet his eyes and pinning me there. "But you're one of us now. We've rehabbed jumpers with broken backs, shattered pelvic bones, concussions—all of which should have been disqualifying, maybe."

When he doesn't say any more, I duck out of his office. I catch a glimpse of the jump list on my way out. My name is at the very bottom, but it's there.

Back in the dorms, I kick the box of Jason's things into the shadows at the back of my closet. I can't bear to look at his stash of Gin Gins, or the damn ukulele. It only makes me weep, and that makes my head pound and my eyes feel like somebody is trying to scrape them out with a wooden spoon.

I keep to myself, mostly. I don't need anyone standing over me while I beat my body back into shape. And I'm not ready for company—not yet.

They put me on duty weeding the flower beds and inspecting chutes in the loft. Somebody tacked Jason's jumpsuit up on the wall in the gear room—the first time I see it hanging there, limp, I sprint outside to puke behind the flowers I've just finished weeding. Someone follows me out there, running their hands down the long muscles of my back, murmuring soothing nothings, but I'm too far gone to even register who it is. My torso heaves, retching long after there is nothing left in my stomach to bring up.

Now I avoid the gear room at all costs.

At odd hours, I find myself frozen in place, my gaze focused on nothing, and only get moving again by the thought of leaving. *I'll just finish sharpening this blade and then I can quit.* But there's always another job placed in my hands when the first one is done. And whatever my heart and my brain have to say about it, my body craves movement. So the miles slide away beneath my feet, and the bulk returns to my arms and shoulders—muscles that had grown soft with disuse hardening again, readying themselves for the work they were trained to do.

When the siren goes off on a Wednesday afternoon, I've moved up to ninth on the jump list. I run to gear up without fully realizing what I'm doing, my stomach flipping and churning more than it ever did on my first jump. I go through the preflight checklist in a fog and load onto the plane with the others. The engine starts and the aircraft lifts into the air. It only takes twenty minutes from the moment the siren goes off until the first stick is dropping through the air.

Griggs is the spotter on duty, and his voice shouting instructions yanks me back to training, when I couldn't see anything through the haze of my own ambition—when grief was some abstract thing that happened to other people. When Jason was still alive.

I'm third in a three-person stick—the last jumper to exit the aircraft. I'm having a hard time getting a full breath. Makes sense, I try to tell myself—the closer you are to the front of the aircraft, and the farther away from the open door at the rear, the less air circulation you'll feel. Still, my mouth gapes as I try to suck in air, but I can't seem to get it down to my lungs. I scrabble at my face mask and tug at the collar of my jumpsuit—suddenly it's all too tight.

The second stick is gone; the plane banks. I can't do this.

The one thing I've always had going for me is confidence. I've always believed that the bigger the challenge, the higher I'll jump to clear it. But that certainty is gone now. I don't trust myself, not anymore.

Griggs shouts the final check with Dirk, the first jumper in my stick. A slap on the shoulder, then Dirk flies. Next is Marsh, one of the veterans, in the door and gone a few seconds later. I should be moving. I should be right behind them.

"Blair!" Griggs shouts, waving me forward. "Get in the door and get your ass out there!"

I can't move.

"Jumper, get in the door!"

I can't.

When I still don't take even one step forward, Griggs slaps his arm across the open door, signaling that he's calling off the jump. He stares at me, hard, then leans into the radio strapped to his shoulder. "Blair has a faulty static line clip; I've refused the jump. You've got an eight-person crew down there. Make it work."

Confirmation crackles over the radio while Griggs watches my face. I back away, shaking from head to toe. I sit in one of the jump seats while the plane turns again, banking lower for the gear drop. Griggs sends the boxes out the door, tracks their descent, then sits opposite me for the whole flight home.

He doesn't say another word. He doesn't have to. A faulty clip—that's what will go on record. But everybody on the ground and everybody back at the base will know the problem was me. If they were at all unsure about whether I was ready to come back, now or ever, well, they've got their answer.

A single flame is more than the yellow crayon that your kindergarten self plucked out of the carton and started scribbling with.

It's white-hot, limned in blue.

It's orange and amber, flickering.

It's the dark zone. At its core, a flame is nothing at all, just an empty pocket of air.

CHAPTER 42

I'M MARCHING TOWARD Hawkins's office to quit when Griggs and Watters ditch their lunch and hustle over to block my path.

"What are you doing?" I try to push around them but they won't let me pass.

"You're not quitting."

"Yes, I am."

"No. You're not."

"Look, if you're worried about how all this reflects on you two as instructors, don't sweat it—I'll tell Hawkins—"

"That's not it."

Watters grabs my shoulders and shakes until I meet her eyes. "I know you blame yourself for Jason, no matter what the investigation concluded. I know you think the guys don't trust you, but I've heard them talking about how you wouldn't leave his body to be burned—how you stayed with him to the end. They respect you."

My head drops. "They shouldn't."

It's all I can get out, except then this moan slides out, betraying me. It feels like fire scorching my throat. And even though my cheeks are running with tears and I'm snotting all over my hands, nothing seems to put out that fire. It burns. It burns so bad.

Watters clamps her arms around me. I drop my head on her shoulder and break—I just break. But Watters only holds on tighter. And then Griggs has his arms around us both. They hang on while the blaze rips through me, gusting and candling, burning me up from the inside out.

It's what Jason would have wanted—for me to finally see that I don't have to face this alone.

That afternoon I go for a run, long enough to leave my emotions in the dust. Then I portion out the calories I know my body needs to recover, and to build back some of the muscle mass I've lost. I sit and make myself eat until every bite is gone. It tastes like dirt and feels like a brick in my stomach, but I eat.

After, I head back to my room. I'll do some weights later, but if I try anything even remotely active now, everything I just choked down is going to come right back up. So I close the door and sit in my dorm room, flinching away from everything in there that reminds me of before.

Like Jason's ukulele, abandoned in the back of my closet. I

can't play the thing—I can barely hold a tune on my harmonica. But I roll off the bed and grab it by the neck, then cross to the window to stare into the glare of sun streaks on dirty glass. I wrap both arms around the soft wood and wish with everything I've got that some last leftover part of him has soaked into the grain and lives there, somehow, still.

Fire Watch-Out Situations

No. 17: Terrain and fuels make escape to safety zones difficult.

CHAPTER 43

AFTER A MEAN bank of afternoon thunderclouds rolls over the Bitterroots to the west, it comes as no surprise to anyone when the siren goes off an hour later. What *is* a surprise, though, is the placement of my name on the jump list—second—sandwiched between Watters and Griggs.

I pull on my gear, zipping all the way down my legs. "I'm not sure I'm ready for this."

"Your pump, sensor, and transmitter are all operating properly?"

"Yes."

"Your endocrinologist is monitoring your levels and Hawkins has approved the system?"

"Yes."

Watters claps me on the shoulder, like a promise—or a threat—that she'll be with me step for step. "You wouldn't be on that list if we didn't trust you to get the job done."

"I don't know . . ."

"Blair. Look at the board. The bottom two dozen jumpers just got back from California. They're here, and they'll jump if we ask them to. But they have earned some time with their families, and their families have earned some time with those jumpers' feet safely on the ground. Marsh is coming with us, but he's a lone wolf. From what I heard over the radio, we'll need all six of us out on that fire. We haven't had rain in weeks. If we don't button this fire up, it's going to get hot fast, and we can't afford that."

Griggs secures his jump helmet, slapping the top for good measure. "What Watters said." He motioned toward the open door. "After you."

I jog toward the plane and the preflight check. I'm straight-up terrified. Not of jumping out of the plane or attacking the fire, but that I'll screw up and someone else will get hurt. Watters and Griggs flank me like cowherds behind a jumpy calf. They must have put my name second on purpose—that's what I get for always leaping to the front of the line during training.

Dammit.

We're loaded on the plane and in the air in a matter of minutes, headed straight toward the plume of smoke. Adrenaline spikes, draining my head of everything else. The spotter lets the streamers fly, and we all crane to watch them ripple toward the ground. I step close behind Watters as the spotter begins his questions for our stick.

"Are you ready?"

No, I'm not. Not even close.

"Ready," she answers.

"Are you tight?"

"Yes."

"Hook up."

We hook our static lines to the cable. The spotter calls out information about the jump spot, streamer drift, elevation, and wind direction. I nod along, clenching my jaw to keep the warring emotions tearing at my insides from spilling out.

"Get in the door." Watters drops to the floor while we perform our final checks.

"Turning final. Three thousand feet. You are clear."

The spotter ducks away from the open door.

"Get ready."

Slap. Watters is gone.

I drop to the step, slapping my hands to either side of my legs, ready to jump. The slipstream tugs at me, playfully, almost. Before my brain can come roaring back with all those doubts and fears, and the impossible weight of grief, I launch myself into the air. I don't even realize I'm screaming until the buzz of the plane fades.

Jason loved this. Every time he jumped, we could hear him whooping with joy from high above. Something wet streaks across my cheeks. With a *snick*, my chute opens above, and the only sound in the whole world is me, sobbing into the open air.

While the rest of me collapses, my body does its work, matter-of-fact, tugging the steering toggles, floating me over the landing spot. I snap my feet together and meet the ground with a practiced roll. I rise up to my knees, unclip, and start rolling the chute to pack it tight. I strip out of my jumpsuit and for the first time, catch the scent of smoke. That smell snaps me back into my body and I look to my right. A thin plume rises straight up, without too much interference from the wind.

Good. The fuel is dry and, now that the thunderstorm has passed, the air is, too. If the wind is kind, we might stand a chance of buttoning this up quick.

"Blair!"

It's Watters.

"Yeah?" I hurry over, ready for my orders, swiping at my cheeks.

"You're making the calls on this one."

"What?" It comes out like a screech, not anything resembling English. "I'm not the JIC, you are."

"That's right, I am. And I want you calling the shots on this fire."

Fear scrabbles at my throat. I can't. My breath starts coming fast, closing off my windpipe. I *cannot* let anyone else down.

I can't do this.

An updraft of cool air finds the back of my neck and wanders across my cheeks, drying any leftover tears.

Old habits; old ways of thinking.

I'm not alone. I failed Jason—the only thing that mattered. I don't have a damn thing to prove. If I *can* do this job, it won't be for myself. The chokehold on my throat releases. I sink back on my heels while the panic rattles out of me.

I turn to find Watters and Griggs watching me while they finish stowing their gear.

"If I'm going to do this, I need your help."

Griggs nods, and Watters blows out a long sigh—is that relief?

"Let's walk and talk."

Tools in hand, we scrabble up to the nearest peak for a good view of the fire. We hike together, fast. At the top, Griggs asks, "Where would you post the lookout?"

I scan the terrain. The fire is burning through the east edge of the meadow—a grass fire, more common to California than Montana, with a big old tree in the middle that the lightning found. "Over there, above that scree slide."

"Good," says Watters. "And exit routes?"

"Along the creek. All the way to the lake if we have to."

Griggs nods in approval. "And?"

"Back the way we came, to the logging road where we'll get picked up."

"Exactly what I'd say." Watters doesn't break eye contact. "And what about containment?"

I release a tight breath, watching the fire begin to crawl across the meadow. "We start at the heel, dig a line around the black, and take that tree down. Then we separate, expanding the line along the flanks, and we try to pinch the head—snuff it out. If we're lucky, it won't get any farther than the creek at the bottom of the ridge."

Watters nods. "Then let's hope we're lucky."

Griggs and Watters start digging while I pass instructions to the guys crossing the meadow at a rapid clip. Yolo takes the first shift as lookout, Marsh begins constructing line, and Dirk gets to work with the saw. Within minutes, the tree struck by lightning is down, being hacked into harmless smolders. Harmless for now, anyway. I glance at the readout on my watch, tuck a gummy into my cheek, and check over my shoulder to confirm the lookout's position.

Then I heft my Pulaski and get to work.

Fire Watch-Out Situations

No. 12: Cannot see main fire;
not in contact with someone who can.

CHAPTER 44

AFTER TWO HOURS, we've buttoned up the heel and split into two groups, with Griggs and Marsh cutting line on the west flank, and Watters and me on the east. The radio chatter has died down, and though the fire is burning hot, the flames are mostly keeping low to the ground. The sawyers take down the few trees that have caught, cutting them into manageable pieces, dispersing and dousing the flames with shovelfuls of dirt.

We work fast and hard, everybody watching the base of the ridge to gauge whether we'll make it there before the flames start racing upward. I hack furiously at the ground, trying to force my nerves to settle.

Instead of sputtering out at the creek like we'd hoped, the fire spits a handful of cinders onto the incline and begins doing what fire loves best, racing uphill. I direct the crew to climb the ridge along the flanks, hemming in the flames. Even if we won't be able to make it around the head to snip it off, I'm hoping we can close it in and find a way to stop it on the other side of the ridge.

But luck is not with us. Wildfire doesn't care if your heart is broken. It doesn't want to hear about fragile rebirths or a newborn's pale, unscorched skin. It's mercurial. Ravenous. Blissfully indifferent.

Halfway up the hillside, the wind picks up, and the visibility goes to shit. It isn't so much a change in direction as a series of gusts rolling through the valley. The radio crackles—it's Yolo.

"You've got a watch-out situation—I'm spotting some flaming debris slopping over your line beneath the crew on the west flank."

I crane my neck to see across the fire, but I can't spot Griggs. Smoke whips past, light shearing off the cliffside and lancing through the trees. I squint, shading my eyes, but it's no good.

"I see it," Griggs reports. "If those flames spread, we'll be cut off from the creek. And if it wraps around the ridge, we won't be able to get back to the logging road either."

My heart bangs in my chest, in counterpoint to my short, startled breaths. "Griggs, gather your crew, abandon your line, and get beneath that fire while you can. We're headed to you."

"Got it."

"Hey!" I call. "We need to reroute—the west flank has been compromised."

Of course my watch pulses right then. I gnash my teeth and force myself to pause, drink some water, and stuff some gummies in my mouth before taking off after the others. I'm furious with myself that it steals even a minute, but I promised Aunt Cate. And Hawkins. And Watters. Hell, I promised myself.

It isn't easy hiking fast with firefighting tools in your hands and all that gear on your back, but we move all the same, flat-out down the ridge, across the meadow, and up the other side to where the fire breached our line.

I'm panting for breath once we get there, trying to hand out new instructions. "Watters, Yolo, you stay below Marsh and me while we put this out. Watch for any sparks or rollout that try to do the same thing to us."

"Got it."

Marsh is a big guy—constantly on a diet to stay a few pounds below the upper weight limit for smokejumpers. Nobody can dig line as fast as him. While he tears up the ground, I settle in a few paces behind, using the Pulaski's flat end to scrape any bits of dry grass out of reach. Well, it *would* be out of reach if the wind would quit it, that is. We get halfway around the new section of fire when Griggs and his crew meet us.

Together we button up the slop. In a matter of minutes, that flank is once again contained. Everybody stops, looking up. The east flank held, at least halfway up, and the line up the west flank is clear now, too, even if it does have an ugly bulge in the middle.

I suck in a ragged breath. "I don't want us separated again.

Let's make one long line, all the way up this flank, everybody watching for debris."

"Makes sense." Griggs nods. "If we hold the west flank and let the east run, it'll hit the Clark Fork before it can reach any towns. It isn't a let-burn area, but the west flank is a critical defense. Watters?"

"Agree."

"If we can beat it to the ridge and at least down a few trees so it can't leap over the other side, that might be the best we can do today." That gets the crew up and moving, and I radio Yolo to watch for the east flank wrapping around the ridge—the last thing we need is another nasty surprise.

After digging for hours on end, I'm sucking wind and fighting cramps in my legs. I've been working on my fitness since I returned to base, but it still isn't at the level it was before. I pay attention every time my watch so much as flickers at me. And I take care of my body so it doesn't become a problem for the team. The line looks good, though, steady up the west flank.

But the wind changes yet again, pushing the flames uphill even faster. We watch, helpless, as fire tears through the trees thirty yards above us. The flames turn that plasticky red that only seems to exist in dollar-store toys, sketchy gas-station candy, and scary-hot fires.

I sink my blade into the dirt and lean against the butt, defeated. We're not going to beat the fire up the ridge. We're just not. And it isn't worth the risk to the crew to keep fighting it.

I gave it everything I had—I tried. I really did. And still, it isn't enough.

Know what your fire is doing at all times.

STANDARD FIREFIGHTING ORDERS, NO. 2

CHAPTER 45

WATTERS TAKES ONE look at my face and stops digging. "You want to call it?"

"If the fire jumps the ridge, that's a box canyon on the other side. We're not going in there."

"So we pack out now?"

I unfold one more section in the map. "Look. The Como fire is only ten miles away. I heard Hawkins listing the engine and handcrews they've got over there. And air support, too. If they could get even one bucket drop to us, we might be able to re-engage this fire."

Watters nods slowly. "It's worth asking."

I unclip my radio, thinking fast. "If they can't, we pack out."

Marsh gets in my face, all two hundred pounds of him. "We can't wait on buckets. Anyway, the crews on the Como can't spare one."

I swallow, hard. "It isn't my job to decide where resources are allocated. It *is* my job to call for help when we need it. And we need help. Right now."

But Marsh won't let up. "I can do it. I can beat the fire up that ridge."

"No." Before, I would have been right there with him, jumping at the chance to prove myself. I fold up the map, looking away from Marsh. "Griggs, hike everybody back to the safe zone."

Marsh is seething, hulking over me. "You're barely a rookie. You can't tell me what to do."

I call in the request for air support, then turn to face him. "You're right. I can't. But your JIC put me in charge and I say nobody is dying today."

The fire is close, hot winds kicking up grit and blasting it across our faces. Marsh stares me down. I wait, breathing hard and staring right back, sweat coursing down my skin. He curses, then nods once, his shoulders, his jaw, every inch of him strung tight.

My radio crackles with static. "Rerouting helicopter oh-ninety-one. Incoming, four minutes."

I turn my back on Marsh so he can't see the radio shaking in my hand. I hunch over so the wind doesn't interfere with the audio, relay the coordinates, then retreat to stand with the others watching the fire.

"Now what?" Yolo ducks close to ask.

"We stay here in the safe zone. We wait. If the bucket hits, we go back in. If not, we pack out, and fast. If anybody reaches their own 'no go' and wants to leave sooner, nobody here will blame you."

Marsh bristles. "I've been jumping for twenty years and I've never, not once, left a fire burning."

Watters steps up, taking Marsh toe to toe. "Then you've been lucky. If today's the day your luck runs out, but we walk out of here, I'd say you're still pretty damn fortunate."

Everybody watches the sky to the east, waiting for that helicopter to come. The fire races uphill, jumping over itself like some sick game of leapfrog. Seconds stretch into minutes. The only sound is fire: whispering, hissing, crackling.

The radio in my hand is slick with sweat.

It isn't all on me.

This isn't all on me.

The team decided to wait for the drop. Okay—so Marsh argued the whole time. But everyone else was with me. I check my watch. Two more minutes until we pack out.

Beside me, Watters and Griggs are steady. He rolls out his neck, shrugging his shoulders to work them loose. Watters systematically repositions the items in her pack, making space to stow extra gear if we have to leave quickly. My team is here; they're ready, and more than capable of stretching the burden across their shoulders.

Marsh huffs. "Okay. We've waited long enough. They're not coming. Face it—"

I throw out a hand, listening. The faint sound of rotors rises above the wildfire's roar. We pivot to watch while a helicopter comes into view. I duck, covering one ear so I can hear the pilot's communication coming in, and confirm the drop.

The helicopter stays high above, where the blowback from its rotors won't fan the flames below. Out of the belly of the craft, a stream of water slaps against the ridgeline. Steam boils upward as the flames are cooled and the helicopter peels away, rerouting to refill and drop again.

A shudder rolls through me. There it is—our fighting chance.

"Back at it?" Griggs offers a weary smile.

I nod. One by one, the crew slaps me on the back or shoulder, or in Marsh's case, the top of my head, then heads out to reengage the fire. Watters is last to go.

"You did good." Through a soot-streaked face, she grins.

"I didn't do it alone."

"You don't have to, not ever."

I nod, my throat too tight to speak. Watters turns away. The radio crackles and I lift it to my mouth. I hesitate before making my report.

"Hey," I call after her.

"Yeah?"

"Thank you," I manage.

"Anytime."

The fire is out before the sun goes down. Back in camp, over the crackle and hiss of slabs of spam roasting over a low campfire, I listen to the crew poke fun at one another, spinning wildly exaggerated stories. I sit back, soaking in the warmth and batting back the urge to push even that small comfort away. If Jason were here, he'd be making jokes and joining in the bluster. If I squint my eyes, I can almost see him there, long legs stretched toward the ring of stones, a goofy smile taking over his whole face.

That night, I sleep with my head outside the open door of my tent. I blink at the speckled black. It's a moonless night—the dark ravenous, devouring light. I'm too tired to think—about Jason or the jump that day—about anything. Though I never knowingly close my eyes, at some point, the darkness consumes even me, dragging me into a dreamless sleep.

If you slice through the trunk of a mature tree, you'll find rings marking the tree's years—everybody knows that. But look closer and you'll notice grooves and nicks in those rings—where the tree was scored by drought, or when floodwaters soaked the roots, turning the earth they clung to sloppy and waterlogged. You'll also find thin black lines—scars—where a fire passed through the stand of trees, licking at the bark and charring the trunk.

As the years pass, those scars are overgrown with new skin, layer upon layer. But the blaze leaves a mark that will never go away.

CHAPTER 46

I LEAN BACK into my camping chair, my neck resting on the double-stitched fabric so I don't have to waste any extra energy holding my own head up. Looking west, orange clouds hunker down over the Bitterroots; a silty sunset is all that's left of yesterday's fire. The wash of color makes me think of Jason—really, everything makes me think of Jason.

The only way to sit with grief like that is to live big and love big, just like he did. Which means it's time to stop avoiding Janie. I sigh and thumb through my missed calls, dial, then listen to the drone of the ringtone. When she doesn't pick up, the call goes to voicemail.

"Hey, Janie. Sorry I ghosted you for a while there—I couldn't deal." I take a ragged breath and try again.

"Look, it wasn't fair to you, and I really am sorry. I know you and Jason were on and off and on again all the time. But you should know that even when you two called it off for a bit, it was always you for him. Jason would have wanted you to be sure about that. He always laid his heart bare for everybody to see—I loved that about him so much."

I grit my teeth so I can keep going. "Anyway, he'd want you to know where you stood with him. He loved you, Janie. Always."

I tap the screen to end the call, squeezing my eyes shut until everything stops spinning. Each time I tackle one of those impossible things, I can breathe a little easier. But every one really is impossible. Next up: sending Jason's little brother, Willie, something from his gear—maybe his hardhat. Then it's time to offer Aunt Cate the world's biggest apology and biggest thank-you for yanking me back when things got too bleak. It'll be easier to breathe once that's said, too.

Maybe tomorrow. Maybe this weekend.

In a little bit, Yolo, Dirk, Watters, and Griggs are going into town for pizza to celebrate that everybody made it out alive yesterday. I'm going, too, and for the first time in a long time, I might even be looking forward to mindless conversation and laughing about pointless shit. But first, a little time to myself.

I glance over to my left arm where, before I left the dorm, I drew a handful of chords in ballpoint pen along the pale skin of my forearm. I glance from the chords to where my hand awkwardly cups the ukulele's neck. The frets are wiggly and my fingertips already sting from trying to scrunch my fingers together to play a

G chord without the strings buzzing. It's one of the great mysteries of the universe how Jason managed it with those fat fingers of his.

I don't try to sing—not because anyone's around to complain about my tone-deaf attempts—it's just, if I'm quiet and if I really listen, I can still hear Jason's voice. And I'm going to hang on to that for as long as I can. Forever, hopefully.

So I hug the instrument to my chest while my left fingertips find their places on the frets. When Jason played, his right hand trilled over the strings—I can barely form the chords, but it's enough, for now. A minor, G, F, then D. I brush over the strings with my right thumb, enough to give the melody somewhere to start from, but quiet, so I can still hear him. Against the shadowed backdrop of distant peaks, the light dims by degrees, orange giving way to rust, scarlet fading to a soft plum. White, then layer upon layer of gray—a sky full of waves lapping the horizon.

I strum as the colors change, as the light turns, listening with everything I've got.

AUTHOR'S NOTE

IN 1997, I worked a summer job for the US Forest Service in Oakridge, Oregon, hiking through forests to map creeks, and snorkeling streams and rivers to count and identify fish species. The previous summer had been a tough fire season for the region; as a preventative measure, and regardless of the fact that we were hired as biologists, not firefighters, my team was put through fire camp. It was an intense training, though compared to what wildland firefighters face on the job day in and day out, it was pretty mild. I finished that summer with a profound respect for work in wildland fire but with no intention to ever work that close to a wall of flame again! Believe me, I had no idea that this visceral experience would still be with me in such a profound way twenty-five years later.

You won't find any teenagers in today's smokejumping crews, though the idea isn't without precedent; a few managed the feat in the 1950s. In truth, the evolution of the smokejumping program, from the first fire jump in 1940 to today's nine bases scattered throughout the West, from the Triple Nickels jumping during the

Second World War to put out wildfires started by Japanese incendiary balloons to covert missions during the Vietnam War, is dramatic enough without any fictive flair. The reality is also that our wildland departments are underfunded, our crews are underpaid, and in recent years understaffed; with the unpredictable volatility climate change carries to the theater of natural disaster, a scenario in which elite crews are dotted with less experienced firefighters is all too imaginable.

The global pandemic we have all endured made the in-person, on-the-ground research I planned for this book nearly impossible. Instead, I poured through memoirs and articles, watched hundreds of hours of video footage, and scoured training manuals and interagency websites. Even so, this novel wouldn't exist if it were not for a few instrumental people who generously shared their experiences in wildland fire with me. Tiffany Demings, Jimmy Dodson, and Lacey England, I am incredibly grateful to have learned from your expertise and insights. Any outstanding errors or omissions are my own.

As someone who has always called the West home, I am indebted to the network of capable, brave, and highly skilled individuals who hold the line between wildfire and the people and places I love. From those who keep fire camps humming to the handcrews cutting line, from those who work behind a desk to those who hike, rappel, or jump into the wilderness: for the lives and wild spaces you protect, thank you. And for every individual working to change fire culture so that people of all genders are treated with dignity and respect, thank you. Your work is critical.

To my young readers living with type 1 diabetes: while the nature of action-adventure books is at times larger than life, and while characters often make terrible personal choices on the page in the name of a good story, the truth is that managing a complex medical condition and prioritizing your own health and well-being is heroic. I'm in awe of the resilience and grit you demonstrate every day just by showing up for yourself.

A book is made by a whole team of people; this time more than ever, I could not have finished this novel without them. Huge thanks to my wonderful editor, Liza Kaplan, and to the fantastic people at Penguin who put this book in your hands: Maria Fazio, Gaby Corzo, Ellice Lee, Krista Ahlberg, Emma Martin, Marinda Valenti, Kristin Boyle, Lori Thorn, Abigail Powers, Sola Akinlana, and Delia Davis. Gratitude, as always, goes to my excellent agent Ammi-Joan Paquette, and EMLA. Thanks to my own personal crew, who lent their support when I needed it most: Megan Benedict, Anna E. Jordan, Cammen Lowstuter, Claudia Mills, Kathy Peterson, Helen Hock, Kristin Sandoval, and Meg Wiviott. Thanks to my sisters, Timme and Chelle. And Mom—I don't think I'll ever be able to hold this book in my hands without remembering our time together this summer. I'm so grateful.

SOURCES

"Firefighting Orders and Watch Out Situations." National Park Service. nps.gov/articles/firefighting-orders -watchout-situations.htm. Accessed October 2021.

"Ram-Air Parachute Training Guide: Equipment Check List." Forest Service, US Department of Agriculture. February 2018. www.fs.usda.gov/sites/default/files/ media_wysiwyg/ratg_final_26feb2018signed.pdf. Accessed October 2021.

"Smokejumpers." Forest Service, US Department of Agriculture. www.fs.usda.gov/science-technology/fire /people/smokejumpers. Accessed October 2021.